Praise for
Kristine Kathryn Rusch

"Rusch is a great storyteller."

—*RT Book Reviews*

"Rusch's greatest strength…is her ability to close down a story and leave the reader feeling that the author could not possibly have wrung any more satisfaction out of the piece."

—*The Kansas City Star*

"Rusch is a great storyteller—easily the equal of Patterson or Koontz."

—*Analog*

"Kristine Kathryn Rusch is one of the best writers in the field."

—*SFRevu*

"[Rusch's] writing style is simple but elegant, and her characterization excellent."

—Mark Morris, *Beyond*

"Kristine Kathryn Rusch's crime stories are exceptional, both in plot and in style."

—Ed Gorman, *Mystery Scene Magazine*

The Early Conundrums

A Spade/Paladin Collection

Kristine Kathryn Rusch

wmg **PUBLISHING**

The Early Conundrums: A Spade/Paladin Collection

"Stomping Mad" by Kristine Kathryn Rusch was first published in *Return of the Dinosaurs* edited by Mike Resnick and Martin H. Greenberg, Daw Books, 1997

"The Case of the Vanishing Boy" by Kristine Kathryn Rusch was first published in *Alfred Hitchcock's Mystery Magazine,* January/February, 2010

"The Karnikov Card" by Kristine Kathryn Rusch was first published in *Alfred Hitchcock's Mystery Magazine,* January/February, 2011

"Pandora's Box" by Kristine Kathryn Rusch was first published in *Alfred Hitchcock's Mystery Magazine,* January/February, 2012

"Trick or Treat" by Kristine Kathryn Rusch was first published in *Alfred Hitchcock's Mystery Magazine,* December 2012

In Memory of Bill Trojan

Contents

The Early Conundrums

A Spade/Paladin Collection

INTRODUCTION

SPADE, THAT Secret Master of Fandom and private detective extraordinaire, made his first appearance in 1997. Mike Resnick asked me to write a story for an anthology called *Return of the Dinosaurs*. I'm really not a big dinosaur fan. I read a lot about dinosaurs at the appropriate age (ten, maybe?) and then I moved on to smaller and more girly things, like horses and unicorns (and boys).

I did what I always do with an anthology invitation: I try to figure out what the other writers will write and then I write something else. Mike developed this anthology in the middle of the *Jurassic Park* craze, so I figured most writers would deal with that (if they set something in the present) or they would deal with actual dinosaurs.

So what did I come up with? A science fiction convention focused on dinosaurs.

I dunno how my brain works, I really don't. It certainly isn't normal, that's for certain.

As I started to write, I realized I didn't have an sf element in the story at all. (In fact, when I sent the finished story to Mike, I told him he didn't need to use it, that I would write him a new story. He used it anyway.) Instead, my main character took over the entire story. Spade, with his opinions, his love of science fiction, his hatred of stupidity, and his uncanny ability to solve crimes, was born.

I wanted to write more about Spade, but with book deadlines and other pressing short story invitations, I never got the chance. Then one afternoon in 2009, I decided that I would go back to Spade, other deadlines be damned.

I wrote "The Case of the Vanishing Boy," and yet another character appeared, fully formed and ready to solve crimes. The pixish Paladin, with her naturally pointed ears and surly manner, tried to steal the story from Spade. But Spade wouldn't let her. Instead, they became mismatched partners, unlikely friends, and the center of a series.

Because, after this, I couldn't let them go. My sf friends, especially those who are Secret Masters of Fandom (no, I didn't make that title up), vetted the stories and made sure I got the convention details right. My good friend, book dealer Bill Trojan, read "The Case of the Vanishing Boy," and gave me a list of all the possible things I could write about Spade and Paladin.

He also came up with a full novel plot that I remember only vaguely. Unfortunately, I didn't write it down, and neither did Bill. He died at the end of the World Science Fiction Convention in August of 2011, leaving a Billsized hole in the universe and tantalizing Spade/Paladin possibilities in my memory. The book is dedicated to him, as all the Spade/Paladin stories will be.

Bill saw all of the stories in this book except "Trick or Treat," which I was going to show him when he got back from Worldcon. He would have liked one part of the story at least: Two of Spade's t-shirts are actual shirts I saw Bill wear.

I have one rule about my Spade/Paladin stories: they can't show sf conventions in a bad light. Yes, bad things happen there (as in every walk of life), but sf conventions are, as Spade says, a haven for those of us who love the genre and see ourselves as just a little bit different.

Spade and Paladin will have many more cases in the future. Some will be the ones Bill suggested; others I have to come up with on my own.

But rest assured that the SMoF and the tough-as-nails investigator will fix whatever problems they run into, one conundrum at a time.

—Kristine Kathryn Rusch
Lincoln City, Oregon
May 15, 2014

STOMPING MAD

S HE CALLED HERSELF the Martha Stewart of Science Fiction, and she looked the part: Homecoming-queen pretty with a touch of maliciousness behind the eyes, a fakely tolerant acceptance of everyone fannish, and an ability to throw the best room party at any given Worldcon in any given year.

So when a body was found in her party suite, the case came to me. Folks in fandom call me the Sam Spade of Science Fiction, but I'm actually more like the Nero Wolfe: a man who prefers good food and good conversation, a man who is huge, both in his appetite and in his education. I don't go out much, except to science fiction conventions (a world in and of themselves) and to dinner with the rare comrade. I surround myself with books, computers, and televisions. I do not have orchids or an Archie Goodwin, but I do possess a sharp eye for detail and a critical understanding of the dark side of human nature.

I have, in the past, solved over a dozen cases, ranging from finding the source of a doomsday virus that threatened to shut down the world's largest fan database to discovering who had stolen the Best Artist Hugo two hours before the award ceremony. My reputation had grown during the last British Fantasy Convention when I—an American—worked with Scotland Yard to recover a diamond worth £1,000,000 that a Big Name Fan had forgotten to put in the hotel's safe.

But I had never faced a more convoluted criminal mind until that Friday afternoon at the First Annual Jurassic Parkathon, a media convention held in Anaheim.

***

The convention was officially called Dinocon I because Crichton's people, or Spielberg's people, or some studio's people wouldn't give permission to use the Jurassic Park name with a non-sanctioned project. I normally don't get involved with a media con, especially one held in Anaheim, but this one had a million dollar budget and a state-of-the-art computer system, and I simply couldn't resist the challenge.

So I was in Ops with most of the folks running the con when the call came through. Ops, for those of you who've never seen one, is a hotel function room with most of the furniture removed, replaced with tables covered with computer equipment, too many chairs, and tons of print out paper. Most of the people working Ops look haggard and stressed by the time the convention starts, and many of them are ready to collapse by the time it's over. So we really didn't need to hear some security person, young by the sound of him, on the two-way radio:

"Hey, ah, we got a, um, Situation X, here."

Everyone in Ops snapped to attention. The actual term was a File X—always a pun, everything a pun—and it was only supposed to be used for an extreme emergency.

"Copy that," Doris, a muscular woman the size of Stallone, said. She headed security, and had at every major con I'd ever worked on. Security is important at sf conventions, perhaps *the* most important thing, because these cons, as most of you know, aren't your simple suit-tie-and-briefcase affairs. The big conventions have three levels: the fans, most of whom dress in costume (some medieval barbarians, some Captain Kirk, some space aliens); the pros, most of whom write, act, or somehow work in the science fiction field; the dealers, most of whom sell sf paraphernalia—books, videos, posters, and the ubiquitous Bajoran earrings. Media cons had more earrings, videos, and actors; fewer books, writers, and intellectual discussions. Behind it all is the con-com, the army of people who run the entire shebang, and put out any and all fires along the way. Security deals with most of those: from regular hotel guests who are scared by the werewolf in the elevator to the teenagers who've stayed up all night playing the card game *Magic*, and who suddenly think it fun to pull the fire alarm on the second floor.

Never, in my twenty years of fandom, have we gotten a call for this kind emergency, and never have I heard a security person sound so scared.

"It's in room 4708. Can someone come here?" The security kid's voice cracked, confirming my suspicion: he was a volunteer, and he was eighteen at most.

"What's the nature of the emergency?" Doris asked.

"I don't think you want me to describe it on an open channel," the kid said.

"All right, be right there," Doris said, and left.

We mused about the "Situation" X for a moment. "Maybe," Ruth, the con chair, said, "he saw a fur bikini for the first time."

"It's the masquerade tonight," John said behind her, and we all laughed. He probably saw a costume, got scared, and decided to call it in. We'd all had that happen before.

"Or maybe it's pea soup," said Ben, and I, being most senior on the staff, groaned. I remembered that one, which had now eased into fannish legend. Just after *The Exorcist* came out, some fans in Baltimore held a room party and served pea soup along with the usual potato chips, cheese, and beer. After midnight, when the crowd got really drunk, someone had the brilliant idea of imitating Linda Blair in the famous vomit sequence. Of course, everyone had to do it, and by the time security arrived, a sea of pea soup was running down the corridor like the Blob without the assistance of the special effects people.

"Please, ghod, anything but that," I said.

At that moment, the phone rang. Ruth answered, and handed it to me, her tired face filled with confusion and surprise. "It's Doris," she said. "For you."

I slid my chair back and grabbed the phone, feeling as confused as Ruth looked. Doris could have radioed me. That would have been procedure. Maybe something was really up in 4708.

"Yeah?" I said.

"Spade," she said—my fannish friends had called me Spade since I solved the first case almost twelve years before—"you've gotta come up here. Now."

"What's going on?" I asked.

"An absolute disaster," she said, and hung up.

"Why didn't she use the radio?" Ruth asked.

I shrugged. "I guess she didn't want anyone else wandering up to the room." I eased myself out of my special chair, the one that I insist a con-com bring to every convention if they want my services, and with a push of a button, shut down the financial files on Dinocon's main computer. Then I made my way slowly—because I never hurry—to the fourth floor of the main convention hotel.

Dinocon had 8,000 registered attendees, and it was only Friday afternoon. The convention was scheduled to go through Sunday, and another 2,000 people were expected at the door on Saturday. Most of these folks were already crowding the halls, having conversations with friends they hadn't seen for a while and trying to discover where that night's parties would be held. I squeezed my way through—negotiating packed hallways was never easy for a man of my bulk—and made it to the elevator in time to nab the last spot. No one complained, though, as I squooshed people toward the back. Part of that was my con-com badge—regular con attendees knew better than to harass a person in a con-com badge—and part of it was my reputation.

"Hey, Spade!" someone yelled from the back. "You get a piece of that diamond?"

"I don't charge for my services," I said, in a gently chiding voice. I made my money years ago as an early employee of Microsoft. I took all my bonuses in stock, and then retired at the age of 31, not as rich as Bill Gates, but rich enough.

"He's a gentleman detective," someone else said from the back, and the entire elevator chuckled.

"Imagine," I said as the doors opened on four, "a gentleman—and a scholar."

I got off, but not before I heard more giggling as the doors closed. Fannish humor was not the stuff of stand-up routines, but it was usually full of sweet, if not always socially adept, affection.

The room 4708 was on what had been designated by the hotel as a party floor. On these floors, it was okay to have loud conversation all night, to serve beer in rooms, and to talk in the hallways. Other floors, the non-party floors, were for people who actually wanted to sleep during the con, something I hadn't done in the last thirteen conventions I had attended.

Photocopied 8"x11" signs were taped onto the wallpaper, most of them announcing bid parties for other conventions. The signs on 4708 looked professionally done on slick glossy paper. They announced the first annual Literature Con to be held in an ancient Hilton an hour outside of Manhattan. I stared at the signs for a moment, frowning. Anyone with half a brain knew that most of Dinocon's attendees weren't likely to attend a literature con, especially one held all the way across the country. But the posters had another draw besides their slick appearance.

Food.

Come to our bid party, the sign read, *and dine at your heart's content. Award-winning chocolates, Lucinda's World Famous Chili, and gourmet dishes from the farthest reaches of the Solar System. Come to* the *party of the convention. You'll talk about it for the next three lifetimes.*

Curiouser and curiouser. Lucinda was Lucinda Danielle Stanhope, also known as the Martha Stewart of Science Fiction. Lucinda hated media cons, thinking that they ruined "pure" science fiction. Pure science fiction, to her, was anything beautifully written with long treatises on science. She thought plot-driven fiction an abomination, and sf on movies and television beneath her notice.

Although she might have changed that opinion, since her current boyfriend, who had started as Science Fiction's answer to James Joyce, had gotten a job as a story consultant for a major studio. ("A guy has to make a buck," he said to me at the last Worldcon. "Besides, since *Independence Day*, everyone is hot for sf properties.")

She might have changed her opinion, but I doubted it.

I had known Lucinda for a long time. She and I had had a run-in at Con Diego (called Con Digeo by its attendees because of all the typos in the program book) several years back and I had tried, unsuccessfully, to avoid her ever since. Our conversations from that day on had consisted of only two words, uttered in passing.

Asshole, she say.

Bitch, I'd respond.

I sighed, squared my shoulders, and braced myself for the verbal onslaught as I knocked on the door.

Doris answered. She looked grim and shaky. She motioned me inside and closed the door.

The suite smelled of fresh bread, chili, and something foul, something I had never smelled before and wasn't sure I wanted to smell again. We stood in an entry that led to the bathroom on the left, a main room just before me, and a bedroom on the right. The security kid so skinny he was skeletal and a shade of green I'd never seen outside of a blacklight poster, leaned against a faux Louis the Fourteenth table. He had a hand over his mouth and was taking deep breaths, as if to calm his stomach.

"What is it?" I asked.

Doris pointed toward the main room. I lumbered in, cautiously, not sure what to expect. A chocolate pterodactyl hung from the ceiling and flower arrangements that looked vaguely prehistoric stood on every end-table, along with cute little origami triceratops heads. A human-sized tyrannosaurus rex made entirely out of cheese stood on a circular mirror stand in the center of the room. Crock pots filled with chili bubbled on a table leaning against the wall dividing the main room from the bathroom.

"What—?" I started to ask again, and then I saw her.

She was sprawled on the floor, her left hand resting on the glass double doors leading out to the patio. The doors were closed. I cautiously made my way around the cheese dinosaur and the main table, still in the middle of preparations for the night's party, and stopped near her apron-clad torso.

There was no doubt it was Lucinda. She wore a linen pantsuit beneath that apron, and in her right hand she held an apple partially julienned into a stegosaurus. It was her head that was the problem.

It had been stomped flat, crushed into unrecognizability. More gray matter than I would have expected spattered the teal carpet, mixed with more blood than I had ever seen in my life. I swallowed twice, hard, not wanting to repeat the pea soup episode and contaminate the crime scene. Then I cautiously made my way back into the foyer.

"You call the cops?" I asked.

"No!" Doris said. "They'd shut us down."

"Damn straight they'd shut us down," I said. "We have a murderer on the loose here."

The kid moaned and headed toward the bathroom.

I grabbed his arm. "Uh-uh," I said. "Puke in the public restroom. You don't want to contaminate a crime scene."

"Too late," he mumbled, yanked free, and stumbled into the bathroom, kicking the door closed behind him.

"Poor kid," Doris said. "I'm amazed he has any stomach left."

"Listen, Doris, we gotta call the cops." I covered my hand with my sleeve and reached for the black rotary dial on the faux Louis the Fourteenth.

Doris put her hand on mine, forcing the receiver down. "It's Friday afternoon," she said. "Think about what that means."

Eight thousand attendees, all of whom would demand refunds. The hotel, which would sue for breach of contract. The reputation, which would shut down all Los Angeles area conventions for the foreseeable future, not to mention all media cons, not to mention all conventions held in this hotel chain forever.

Millions of dollars, all because Lucinda made someone stomping mad.

"Can't we at least wait until tomorrow?" Doris asked.

Retching sounds echoed from the bathroom. My stomach rolled in sympathy.

"Tomorrow?" I asked. "Don't you remember the party signs that are up all over this convention. For tonight? In this room?"

"Can't we change them to tomorrow night?" she asked. "Then we won't have to refund, and we won't be in breach of contract."

But we would still have the reputation problem, along with another one. "Tampering with a crime scene is illegal, Doris," I said softly.

"Can't you solve this?" she asked. "Can't you solve this before the cops get here?"

"I've never done a murder investigation before, Doris," I said.

"*Please,*" she asked. "If we can give them a suspect, they won't shut us down, and Ruth and I can handle the PR problem, at least long enough to save the con."

"You don't care that a woman has been trampled in her own hotel room?"

Doris crossed her muscular arms. "You really need to ask me that, Spade? I wouldn't be so rude as to ask you."

She could have, though. Because I was upset. Lucinda had her points. She made a mean chocolate soufflé, and she knew more about fannish foods than anyone I had ever met. She also had her moments: the charity auction she ran for literacy at Orycon in the early '90s brought in $5,000 more than usual because she browbeat the attendees into spending more money. And she got them to do it by having them buy signed books.

Sometimes I found myself in complete agreement with Lucinda's arguments.

And that terrified me.

I stared at Doris.

"Will you help us?" she asked.

I sighed. "I won't tamper with the crime scene, and I will meet with the police when they arrive. You will call them from this room and you will make sure that no one else enters here. You'll also keep the kid from talking to anyone but me. If I happen to solve this thing before the police arrive, fine. But I won't go any farther than that. I'm not going to let some murderer run loose because you want to hold a media con honoring one of the lamest movies of all time."

"The special effects were cool." The kid had opened the door to the bathroom. He was now a chalk white.

"But the plot sucked," I said. Then I nodded at Doris. "Call. I'm going to snoop a bit. And don't leave until I tell you to. Got that?"

She nodded and reached for the phone. I stopped her. "Cover your hands with your sleeves. And don't touch anything besides that receiver."

She glared at me, but followed my instructions. I prowled into the bedroom, deciding to talk to the kid after his breath cleared up.

Lucinda, not surprisingly, was a neat freak. She had arrived and unpacked, her clothing hanging on her hangers in the walk-in closet. Each item was separated by tissue paper, and her hats were in boxes on the shelf above. Her shoes were lined up below in neat little rows beneath the matching clothes. She had two wigs on the dressing table, one studded with little plastic dinosaurs—the clear brightly colored kind that bartenders used to put in drinks in the mid-sixties. A silver lamé dress hung from the plant hook in the ceiling. Lucinda had planned to go all out on this party, and it surprised me. She had to be doing a favor for someone. Media cons were beneath her—and while she enjoyed fannish cooking, she hated fannish clothing.

I got back into the foyer as Doris hung up the phone. "I didn't tell them it was a murder," she said.

I mentally shook my head. That would be her problem when the cops arrived. It would be better for all of us if I had some idea what had happened.

"Okay, kid," I said to the security boy, "come into my office and talk to me. And don't touch anything."

The kid's color still hadn't returned. He followed me into Lucinda's bedroom and started to close the door.

"Don't touch," I said. We went deep into the bowels of the room, and stopped near the bed. I knew that Doris would have trouble hearing us from this spot because I had had trouble hearing her on the phone.

"What's your name?" I asked.

"Chad," he said. I raised a single eyebrow, Spocklike. I had never met a kid who worked con security named Chad. Or at least, a kid who worked con security who would admit to being named Chad.

"Okay," I said, "I need to know: what made you come to this room in the first place?"

He wiped his mouth with the back of his hand. That stomach of his was amazingly weak. "I was by the flyer table—that was my post—when these fans came down the stairs and told me they'd heard a huge pounding on the fourth floor. They took me to their room on three and I heard it too, like something really heavy was going to crash through the floor. Then I came up here. The door was open, and I let myself in. It was really quiet. I called out to see if anyone was here, and then I saw the food. I went in to grab a snack and —"

He burped, then covered his mouth, swallowing hard. "Sorry," he said.

"It's all right," I said. "Do you know who these fans were?"

"Not by name," he said. "But they have the room below this one."

And were probably preparing for another party since the room below also had to be a suite. I rubbed my chin in proper detective fashion. I had a conundrum. I need to talk to those fans, but I didn't want to leave Doris alone in the room. Nor did I want anyone else to know what had happened to Lucinda.

Then I realized it didn't matter. Doris had been in the room without me already. I had investigated, and I knew how things looked. I had seen everything but the bathroom, and that could be remedied.

I took the kid back to the foyer. "Wait here," I said, and peered into the bathroom. The kid had already contaminated the crime scene—several times—but there didn't seem to be much to see. The bathtub was still maid-spotless and the counter had Lucinda's make-up and nothing else. The toilet seat was up, one of the towels was askew, and otherwise everything looked fine. It didn't even smell as bad as I thought it would.

"Okay," I said as I emerged. "Let's find those fans. You wait here, Doris, and don't touch anything."

"Don't worry," she said, looking faintly annoyed at the suggestion.

The kid and I slipped into the hallway. The con was filling up. Two women wearing belly dancer skirts and midriff tops, conversed about the proper navel jewel. Five teenage boys compared tattoos. Three grown men, in Klingon boots and armor, adjusted each other's forehead ridges.

The kid and I took the stairs.

The third floor was filled with people in dinosaur costumes. Some were cheap Halloween masks, while others were full-bore papier-mâché or plastic. The costumes looked heavy, they looked hot, and they smelled of glue. I stared at them, mostly at the feet, wondering what kind of pressure a person would need to drive those hard plastic soles through a skull and crush it.

Then we were in front of 3708. The kid knocked on the door. His hand was shaking.

It was opened by a slender woman whose black hair formed perfect Louisa May Alcott ringlets around her face. She wore a lavender satin shirt with purple satin pants, and the outfit somehow looked perfect on her. Her convention badge was clipped to a tiny piece of cardboard inside her shirt's high pocket, so as not to ruin the satin.

"Hi," she said, looking a bit confused.

"Security," the kid said, glancing at me. "Remember? You asked about the big stomping?"

"Oh, yeah." She was staring at me. Her eyes were lavender, like the shirt. I'd never seen eyes like that in person before. Only in photographs of Elizabeth Taylor. "Who're you?"

"I'm from Ops," I said. "Mind if we come in?"

"Why?" She was asking the kid.

"Because when I went upstairs," he said, "I found —"

I kicked him. He shut up.

"He found that he had a few more questions to ask you," I said. "Mind if we come in."

"No," she said. "I guess not."

She got out of our way, and we stepped into the foyer. It exactly matched the suite above, only here the carpet was brown. Two men sat in the suite's living room. They looked vaguely familiar. They stood as they saw us come in.

"Something wrong?" the first one asked.

He was tall and muscular—those fakey kind of muscles that come from too much health club, and too much low-fat food. His shirt was unbuttoned below the navel, revealing a washboard stomach, and his bare feet looked manicured. His companion wore ripped jeans and a *Star Trek* t-shirt, but unless I missed my guess, his hair had been permed.

Interesting look, for fans. It looked a little too Hollywood, a little too put together, for my tastes. Maybe these folks were slumming.

"You guys with the convention?" I asked.

"What's this all about?" T-Shirt asked. He had his hands on his hips. Same fakey muscles, and he didn't look as if he had ever cracked a book. But, I reminded myself, this was a media con. Folks here didn't have to crack books, even though most of them did.

"Of course we're with the convention," the woman said, and tugged gently on her badge as if to prove it.

"What's your interest?" I asked. "Filking?"

"Excuse me," Manicured asked. His face flamed and he looked insulted.

"Fill-king," the kid said, "not fucking."

Interesting comment, I thought, but I didn't look at him. "Pipe down, Chad," I said. "What are you guys doing at the con?"

"Anyone can come," the woman said, apparently realizing that my questions had more importance than the guys were giving them credit for. "Right?"

"Of course," I said, "but usually people have special reasons for attending. What are yours?"

"We like dinosaurs," T-Shirt said.

"Fascinating," I said in my best Spock voice. No one laughed, even though most fans usually did. My best Spock voice was pretty damn good. "So what's your favorite dinosaur? A plugosaurus or a brontodacdyl?"

"All of 'em," T-Shirt said.

"Hmmm," I said. "Hear you had some noise problems."

"Yeah, man, sounded like weird pounding upstairs," Manicured said. "Like someone was trying to punch a hole in the floor."

"Sounds serious," I said. "Will someone move that chair over here?" I pointed to a square wooden chair that seemed to be the sturdiest thing in the room. T-Shirt moved the chair to the place I pointed to, right next to the balcony doors.

"Spot me, Chad, will you?" I asked as I climbed up.

"Ah, um, ah, you might want me to do that," he said.

"No need," I said, even though the chair was groaning under my weight. I reached up and removed the ceiling panel. Gobs of dust and dirt rained on me, and I had to clear a spider web, but after that I had a pretty good glimpse of the space between the ceiling and the floor above.

"Looks normal," I said, and to my surprise, it did. I put the tile back. "You guys are safe."

"That's it?" the woman asked. "That's all? It sounded wretched up there."

"It was," Chad said. I braced myself on his shoulder and squeezed as I got down. It shut him up again.

"That's it," I said cheerfully. "I hope you have a good con."

"Ah, thanks," T-Shirt said. He was frowning at me.

The kid and I left. The dino costumes flooded the hall. The newer ones looked even more realistic than the earlier ones. Especially the Spielbergian velociraptors. All terrifyingly icky except for the guy wearing blue jeans and a tie-dye brontosaurus head. And the inevitable tot dressed as Barney.

One glance at the elevator told me we weren't going back to the fourth floor that way. Too crowded. It also meant the cops wouldn't come up very quickly when they arrived.

"Where to now?" the kid asked.

I didn't answer. I was feeling pretty annoyed with him. Pretty annoyed with the whole thing, really. I wanted to get back to my Ops computer with its lovely numbers and forget I had ever gotten involved with this detecting business.

Even if I was good at it.

We took the stairs and I was puffing by the time we reached the fourth floor. I hadn't had this much exercise in weeks. And I was moving faster than I liked.

Most of the dino costumes were on the third floor. Regular con-goers littered the fourth. None of them looked like the three ringers downstairs.

I shave-and-a-haircut knocked on 4708. Doris answered immediately. "What took you so long?"

I didn't answer. As I came in, I asked, "Did Lucinda know I was coming to Dinocon?"

"How should I know?" Doris asked.

I glared at her.

She sighed, exasperated. "Probably. If she was looking. You would have been hard to miss since your name was in the con-com listing in all the progress reports. Why?"

I had my suspicions. I made my way back into the suite's main room.

"Hey!" the kid said. "What're you doing?"

His voice had gotten increasingly shrill. I ignored him. I made my way to the body, and, just as I remembered, the floor didn't sag under my considerable weight.

I knelt beside the body. The gray matter and blood were drying in a perfect arch.

"Hey!" the kid yelled. "You said no tampering."

"Grab him, Doris," I said through my teeth. He was getting on my nerves. This whole thing was.

I grabbed the right wrist, dislodging the julienned stegosaurus, and felt—plastic. Soft, lifelike, fake plastic.

"Bitch," I mumbled. I half expected the crushed dummy to mumble "asshole" in return. Then, louder, I said, "Doris, did you call 911?"

She didn't answer. I turned. She was frowning at me. "Doris?"

She flushed. "No," she said. "I called the regular line. I wanted to give you as much time as possible."

Her caution had worked to our advantage. "Call and cancel," I said. "Then break that kid's arm if he doesn't tell you where Lucinda is."

"Lucinda —!"

"Just do it." First time I'd ever understood the sense of a Nike ad.

She twisted the kid's arm up behind his back. Within seconds, he was screaming, "Executive Suite! Executive Suite!"

I got up and walked over to him. "Key," I said.

He handed me a specially marked executive floor key. "Come on, Doris," I said. "Keep a good grip on this kid and commandeer us an elevator."

She did exactly as she was told.

***

On the way up, I explained the whole thing, and the kid wisely said nothing, confirming all my suspicions. I was trying to contain my anger, because this thing had just become personal.

And to think I would have mourned the bitch if that had truly been her on the floor below.

You see, the plan was simple: the execution was hard. Lucky for Lucinda that her boyfriend had his new job in Hollywood and even luckier for her that most special effects guys are also sf nerds. Ironic that she needed media people to tamper with a media con. But Lucinda had always been a bit dim when it came to irony.

And, apparently, detail, at least non-food related detail.

First there was the fannish clothing. No matter what kind of theme party Lucinda gave, she never, ever dressed in fannish clothes. No wigs decorated with little plastic dinosaurs, no silver lamé dress. She might have consented to work a media con, but she would never have given up her stylishly proper clothing. She planned the perfect media party, all right, down to the clothes, forgetting that she would never, ever wear those clothes because, of course, she didn't plan to.

But that wasn't the only detail that bothered me. The three "fans" on the floor below had been extras in a straight-to-video sf release that I'd been watching at home a few nights before the con. I would have made them as non-skiffy folk anyway. All science fiction fans—media and lit alike—know the difference between a real dinosaur and a made-up one.

And then there was Chad, clearly another actor for hire. Except he overdid the vomit bit, and the bathroom smelled as if the maid had just left. Lucinda probably hadn't counted on the strength of my sniffer.

But she had counted on me. In fact, I had been the center of her plan. Without me, it wouldn't have worked. She knew that I knew better than to tamper with a crime scene, no matter how great the temptation. She knew that I had a healthy respect for the authorities and that I would insist on cops being present.

And she knew that the cops would see this for the hoax it was. She would appear at the right moment, blame the convention for overreacting to her little party, piss off the cops just enough to get the whole con shut down. The hotel chain would have been angry, the attendees would have demanded refunds, and the whole cascade effect that Doris had foreseen when she first saw that body would have occurred. Media cons, not just in LA, but all over the country would have suffered, and possibly died.

Lucinda's little stunt would have caused more damage than the murder. It was sabotage, served cold.

***

When we reached the executive suite, Doris made the kid open the door. Lucinda saw him, stood up, and cooed. She was dressed for her act in a white sheath that accented her lightly tanned skin and golden hair.

When she saw us, her eyes widened.

"You bitch," Doris said, blowing my line and letting go of the kid. He started to back away, but I shoved him forward and closed the door behind us.

"Back off, Doris," I said. "She's mine. There won't be any cops, Lucinda. You won't ruin this convention."

"I'm going to see that you're banned from cons forever. I'm going to make sure that your name is taken out of the Fannish Directory. I'm going to —"

"For what? For a little party I planned to throw for some friends?" Lucinda asked. "Don't you think it rather cute? I do."

"You —"

Doris lunged for her, and I caught her, staggering a bit under her power.

The kid bee-lined for the bathroom, fear making his intentions real this time.

"Go to Ops," I said to Doris. "Tell them everything is fine. I can take it from here."

"I'm going to get you," Doris said, but she listened to me. She knew as well as I did that strange things happened at sf conventions, and that there was no proving malicious intent here.

Knowing about it was something else.

"Misunderstandings are so tragic, Doris," Lucinda said, blinking her blue eyes guilelessly.

Doris growled and disappeared out the door. I stood in front of Lucinda. "Media cons aren't your style."

She smiled. It was sweet as rhubarb pie. "They're not yours either."

"I don't see anything wrong with people having fun. I'm a bit more open-minded than you, Lucinda. I believe people can enjoy reading and watching movies. I believe there's room in fandom for both."

"You're so naive," she said. "These cons are so anti-literature. They appeal only to the ignorant. People who don't understand real science, or real science fiction."

"I think people who think they guard pure science fiction may not understand real science or real science fiction either," I said pointedly.

"Good god," she said, "a philosophical discussion when I have a party to finish."

"It seems strange to me that you'd put on a party here, Lucinda."

She shrugged. "I thought I'd give these people the opportunity to come to a lit-con and see what they were missing."

"So kind of you," I said.

She smoothed her dress. "We all do what we can in the circumstances provided."

At that moment, I almost told her what tripped her up. I almost told her that it was her lack of scientific knowledge, her lack of understanding of forensic science that had destroyed her. First, the splatter had been too pretty, too uniform. Second, and more importantly, the type of force it took to stomp out someone's brains would have caused damage to the plywood floor. Damage someone of my weight would have felt in loose boards or groaning wood.

But I didn't. Why give her the ammunition? She might try again someday.

"Am I excused?" she asked brightly.

"There is no excuse for you, Lucinda," I said in my best fannish manner, and moved out of her way.

***

The bane of the non-licensed investigator is that we have no real authority. We can't arrest. Worse yet, people with authority often look down their noses at us.

So we are forced to take some matters into our own hands.

Lucinda, misguided as she was, was clever. Who could prove that the panic the kid, Doris and I felt was anything more than a product of our own imaginations? She would say that she had planned a perfect party, and we had nearly ruined it.

In fact, that night, she did carry off the party with full aplomb. She did change the victim from her clone to that of a lawyer, in keeping with *Jurassic Park* (the movie) tradition, and she did pour ice in the bathtub, but those were the only changes she made. The party was the hit of the convention, and became the talk of sf—both media- and literature-oriented—for years to come. It was, in its own way, the Woodstock of science fiction. Eventually everyone who was anyone claimed they had been there, even if they had been clear across the country at the time.

Everyone who was anyone except me.

You see, I was in Ops, checking the computer records. We had an unexplained power failure just as I was transferring Lucinda's credit card information from her con file into an active file so that we could bill her account. Unfortunately, the accident caused blips in her credit record that cascaded down the system and destroyed her credit rating for the next year. She had to defend and deny and repair, all of which took time away from cons and con parties, and fandom.

And somehow she got it in her pretty little head that this would happen again if she ever attempted to sabotage—even accidentally—a major convention again.

Misunderstandings are so tragic.

But we all do what we can in the circumstances provided.

THE CASE OF THE VANISHING BOY

*D*AY TWO OF FleshCon and Con Ops already smelled like sweaty feet, stale potato chips, and rancid Coke. I expected it. By day two of a science fiction convention, the folks in convention operations had already been working 24/7 for five days straight. We might not have moved our headquarters to the hotel until the day before the convention began, but by then we were already exhausted, cranky, and surviving on too little sleep.

FleshCon isn't as lurid as it sounds. Hosted in a Hilton-wannabe on the outskirts of Lake Tahoe, FleshCon was originally called CannibalCon in honor of the Donner Party. It was designed as a straight science fiction convention, with a masquerade, a literary track, a media track, and an entire wing set aside for gaming.

But the organizers of CannibalCon learned a sad truth about names: No one wanted to come to a convention that celebrated chowing down on human flesh.

FleshCon, on the other hand, sounded like a porn convention. And even though parents balked at sending their kids unchaperoned, the con's new name had the rather fortuitous effect of bringing in new attendees. Once they'd paid their money and gotten their badges, they usually stayed for at least one programming item and one long tour of the dealer's room.

Some even came back for the rest of the convention.

I thought that a great victory, but I'm a great promoter of science fiction conventions. I spend my weekends running conventions all over the country. I am, in fannish lingo, a SMoF—a Secret Master of Fandom.

Fandom is, by definition, made up of the people who attend science fiction conventions. Or if your definition is wider (like mine is) Fandom is composed of the people who read science fiction and fantasy novels, or watch science fiction and fantasy movies, or play science fiction and fantasy games. In other words, most of America belongs to Fandom—they just don't know it yet.

My job is to convince them to join our little club. Sometimes I do that through public speaking, and sometimes it's through my convention work.

I can do all of this because once upon a time, I took an offer that the great Bill Gates offered the employees of his then-fledgling corporation, Microsoft. He gave us the choice to be paid in full in cash or in part in Microsoft stock. As Microsoft grew from a small Seattle corporation to a global international giant, those of us who took the stock options became rich damn near overnight.

We were Masters of Our Own Destiny. We quit our jobs because our stock interest in Microsoft had vested and we were now worth a lot of money. In the Pacific Northwest, people still call us Microsoft Millionaires.

Now, decades later, a lot of the Microsoft Millionaires have become the Microsoft Poorionaires. But there are still a handful like me, folks who knew how to manage money. I took my Microsoft millions and parlayed them into even more millions.

I'm not worth as much as Paul Allen, Bill Gates' initial partner in crime (and founder of the Science Fiction Museum in Seattle—making him, yes, you got it, a member of Fandom). But I am worth a lot. My goal is to turn my tens of millions into hundreds of millions before I turn sixty-five.

But that's a personal goal, one I don't talk about often.

Nowadays, I indulge my hobby, flying across the country, helping conventions in trouble get back on track or setting up systems at young conventions like FleshCon, making sure they'll survive in the Brave New World of the 21st century.

Besides, I like being a SMoF. It gives me more pleasure than all of my Microsoft Millions compounded at a 20 percent annual rate. I've met all of my favorite authors, most of my favorite television stars, and even a few of my favorite movie stars.

Mostly, though, I spend time with the hardcore fen. We speak the same language—like the word fen which, in Fandom, is the plural of fan, or the word filking which is sf's version of folk singing (with sf lyrics). We're proud to call ourselves geeks. We provide a safe haven for the strange, the different, and the too-intelligent-for-their-own-good.

I love the haven. I love the conversations. And most of all, I love saving a convention for the future—making sure that it will roll around on the very same weekend in the next year, providing that safe haven year-in and year-out.

Science fiction fandom saved me from a lifetime of loneliness. It taught me social skills (kinda, sorta—the fen are not known for their social aptitude), gave me a place to go besides my imagination when things were really bad at home, and kept me from hiding in my basement.

It was the same kind of outlet provided by the books I read, the same kind of outlet that the good conventions are for kids even now. I want to preserve that.

We all need an escape.

I just choose to live in the heart of mine.

***

So, back to FleshCon 2 and the smell of sweaty feet. By day two, Con Ops looked like a war zone. A stack of hotel chairs near the door had toppled. The fake wood tables near the walls were covered with paper, badges, schedules, programs and the daily con newsletter, as well as every snack known to man. Too many laptops fought for recharge space on too few electrical outlets, and the four big convention computers—still the old PCs with gigantic towers of terror—dominated the tables lining the back wall. Security's cameras—a new addition since some of the scandalous cons of the late 1990s—and the ubiquitous walkie talkies covered another wall.

I always carve my workspace out of the corner between security and data operations. I bring my own Tower of Terror as well as two laptops, since my usual job is convention finance.

Believe it or not, these conventions are multimillion dollar operations. Or, to be more precise, some conventions are multimillion dollar operations. If the con isn't set up right to start, then it implodes under its own weight.

Since most cons are generally held in hotel chains these days, implosions reverberate throughout the country. Stiff one Hyatt-Regency and the entire chain looks askance at any sf con who wants a booking.

I'm the guy who tries to prevent these disasters.

But that's not my only function.

Since the mid-1990s, I have acted as in-house detective. I have solved more crimes than the now-retired Gil Grissom on *CSI*, Leroy Jethro Gibbs on *NCIS*, and Don Epps on *NUMB3RS*. I'm not up to Perry Mason's level, but I'm working on it.

That's why, at sf cons, people only know me by my nickname.

Spade.

That's for the real Sam Spade—the one made famous in the movies by Bogie. My Humphrey Bogart imitation would be perfect if you turned out the lights and listened to me speak. Turn them on and you know that the short, hard-smoking, long faced man of film fame and I have only our voices in common.

I'm 6'6", nearly 400 pounds, and smoke-free.

I also hadn't yet found my Lauren Bacall.

Not that I'd been looking. I figured no great beauty would ever flirtatiously teach me to whistle, let alone fall in love with this mug.

Which was why I always looked askance at pretty women. Even pretty women who somehow found their way to a science fiction convention.

***

At the crack of dawn on day two, which at an sf convention is 8 a.m., I wandered into Con Ops with my double chocolate espresso and a box of two dozen donuts from the Donut Hut next door. I headed directly for my chair. I had four chairs specially made for my frame and I always shipped one ahead of each convention.

The other SMoF s called my chair the Captain's Chair—a reference to Captain Kirk's chair in the original *Star Trek* (because he always glared at anyone who used his chair—and damn if I don't glare at folks who use my chair as well). My chair has more buttons and knobs than the engine room of a Navy Destroyer.

Captain's Chair indeed.

I was the first person in Con Ops who arrived to replace the night crew. The night crew looked even more haggard than they had when I left. Three people, two men and a woman, wearing jeans and FleshCon 2 t-shirts (all one size too small), sat in front of the main computer towers. All three leaned their cheeks on one fisted hand while the other hand tapped something on the keyboard in front of them.

"Good morning!" I said as cheerfully as I could. Cheerfulness annoyed most fen, particularly at eight in the morning.

All three volunteers jumped at the sound of my voice. One of the men, who had been introduced to me as Pat From Reno, actually looked frightened.

Then he glanced at my chair.

The women looked down. I set the donuts on the snack table against the wall, but kept a firm grip on my espresso.

Then I walked slowly, deliberately, to my chair.

As I did, Pat From Reno said, "She won't leave."

A cold chill went down my back. I didn't see legs dangling from my chair or an elbow hanging over the armrest. But I knew the "she" that Pat From Reno referred to had to be in or near that chair.

I grabbed the thick leather headrest and spun the chair toward me.

"She" was sitting cross-legged in the center of the seat, so small and slender that I initially thought I was looking at a child. Then I realized that no child would grin at me like that, with a mixture of mischief and daring, and just a hint of good old-fashioned sensuality.

She wore Capri pants, flat sneakers, and a t-shirt with a Thomas Canty painting of a knight spread over her small but rather delicious breasts.

"That's my chair," I said. "No one sits in my chair."

She shrugged one shoulder, then tucked a strand of her long blond hair behind her right ear. It was tiny and faintly pointed on its top—what I had once described to a friend of mine as the ideal science fiction fan ear because it could, when wedded with the right masquerade costume, make its owner look like an elf.

She was small enough to be an elf. Her features were delicate enough, except for her luminescent eyes. But I doubted elves wore gold rings on every finger and filigree sword earrings with the hilts curving around the ear lobe.

"*I'm* sitting in your chair, and I'm someone."

Her voice was musical but firm. A soprano with a touch of alto. Someone who knew how to use her vocal richness to charm and beguile.

"In fact," she added, "I slept in your chair. It's quite large, you know."

My face warmed. I hadn't blushed since Keira Knightly at her one and only ComicCon had taken my hand and curtsied in front of me, saying in her delightful British accent, *Such a pleasure to finally meet the famous Spade.*

She probably confused you with David Spade, said a friend of mine later.

Yeah, I quipped. *Because I'm the thin and wiry type.*

"The chair," I said, mostly because I was shaken, "is not made for sleeping."

Her eyes narrowed playfully. "You're telling me the great Spade has never fallen asleep in his own chair?"

The great Spade had fallen asleep in his own chair many times and awakened later, his face pressed against the keyboard in front of him, the side of his mouth covered with drool.

"The great Spade," I said, "is cranky without his caffeine and would like to sit down."

"All you had to do was ask." She placed her tiny hands on the arm rests and levered herself out, keeping her legs crossed until she had balanced her torso over the ground.

People at science fiction conventions—*women* at science fiction conventions—were not usually able to leverage themselves out of a chair, let alone remain cross-legged while they supported themselves with their arms.

She grinned at me, then leaned against the table, her long fingers uncomfortably close to my keyboard.

I sat down heavily and, to my shame, grunted as I did so. The entire chair shook. It didn't want my weight, not after hers. The leather smelled faintly of jasmine, and I realized that had to be her scent.

"What makes you think you can sit in my chair?" I asked.

"*Sleep* in your chair," she corrected with a grin.

"*Be* in my chair," I said, not willing to take her lead. I knew I was sounding grumpy. I *was* grumpy. I'd learned long ago there was no point in charming pretty women. They all saw me as a tall lurching fat guy who could be a good resource or a great pal, but never ever as the romantic lead.

Of course, I never saw myself as the romantic lead either.

"I liked *being* in your chair," she said, and the way she emphasized "being," she made it clear she was playing off both of its meanings. She liked sitting in my chair and she liked existing in it.

In spite of myself, I was beginning to like her—and not in a great pal kinda way.

"Well," I said even more grumpily. "You weren't invited to be in my chair and you're not part of Con Ops, so you need to leave."

"No, I don't," she said, tapping those rings against the edge of the table. "I came here to talk to you."

I sipped my espresso. It had too much chocolate and not enough coffee.

"So talk," I said.

Her fingers stopped tapping. "I'd like to hook up."

I nearly did a spit-take. Only the idea that I would have sprayed espresso all over her stopped me.

Since I was choking, Pat From Reno spoke for me. "Hook up? With Spade?"

I didn't need the disbelief in that last word, although I probably would have put more disbelief into it myself.

"Hook up with him on a case," she said, giving Pat From Reno a cold glare, one that clearly communicated that he was not part of this conversation.

Then she turned back to me, and her eyes became warm again.

She extended her right hand. "Maybe you've heard of me. Folks around these parts call me Paladin."

My breath caught. I had heard of someone named Paladin, but I had always assumed it was a man. In fact, I figured he was some slightly nutty fanboy who had found illegal dups of *Have Gun, Will Travel*, the once-popular Western television show from fifty years ago. Richard Boone played Paladin, a jack-of-all trades who offered his services for hire out of some saloon in San Francisco. The show got into some weird copyright troubles and wasn't aired for decades.

(And the fact that I can pull such details off the top of my head is why sf fans hire me. I notice and remember detail. I also am a repository for way too much useless information. Which is probably why I am so large.)

"Paladin," I said with all the sarcasm I could muster. "No one ever said Paladin was a girl."

"People talk about me?" she asked.

Yeah, they did, in those hushed tones folks used when they were impressed or talking about something they didn't entirely believe in. I knew someone named Paladin existed in the convention circuit. I just never believed the actions attributed to Paladin—taking down an art dealer who was selling fake limited edition prints, finding and capturing (single-handedly) a slippery identity thief who specialized in breaching the best con computer systems, and of course, the most important story to fen, finding a kidnapped Chihuahua (a famous Chihuahua, one that had won many masquerade contests all by its lonesome) and preventing any harm from coming to its very famous doggy self.

"*The* Paladin?" I asked.

"Well, no. Not really," she said. "Technically, there is no *the* Paladin. Even if you go back to the word's origin, which comes from Charlemagne's court, you'll see that there were initially twelve—"

"Peers," I said. "They were called the Twelve Peers of Charlemagne's Court. Over time, the word Paladin, which literally means an officer of the palace, became tied with the idea of any well-known hero—"

"Or knight errant," she said. "I prefer the knight errant version myself."

We were out-geeking each other and we knew it. Wordplay, intellectual one-up-manship, and I-know-more-than-you-do games had been around as long as fandom had. We were speaking the language of our people.

And that, more than her Tom Canty t-shirt, convinced me that she was a member of the fen, which automatically made me more comfortable with her.

She reached into the back pocket of her Capri pants and pulled out a business card. Without even looking at it, I knew what it was. It would say in fine old West script:

Have Gun, Will Travel
Wire Paladin
San Francisco

Only it didn't. What it actually said was:

Have Gun, Will Travel
E-mail Paladin@paladinsanfrancisco.com

"So this is the version for the new century," I said. "What are you? A shill for a revival of the TV show?"

Her cheeks flushed and her eyes glittered. My tone had finally made her mad.

"I work as hard as you do," she snapped. "Maybe harder, since I don't have Microsoft Millions to keep me happy. I heard you were good. That's why I'm seeking you out. I need your expertise."

I took another sip, not even tasting the espresso. I was just hiding behind the giant disposable cup with the Starbucks quote of the day stamped all over its side.

With my free hand, I extended the card to her. "I work Con Ops all over the country. I sit in front of computers all day. It's work, but it's fun. You don't need me. You need someone like me."

"You solve mysteries," she said, refusing to take her card back. "I've got one I can't solve on my own. And I thought the great Spade could help me out. Guess I was wrong."

I should have tossed her card at her. I should have swiveled my chair away from her and told her that I had waaaay too much work to keep FleshCon running, that I had an obligation.

But of course I didn't.

Because she had used the word "mystery," and damned if that word didn't get me every single time.

Particularly when it was spoken by a dame.

***

We needed to go somewhere private, so I walked her to the hotel's restaurant.

It was one of those large sprawling restaurants that covered half of the lobby. The restaurant was one of the few features I liked about this hotel—you could have privacy while eating, yet still see everyone passing by.

As we stepped out of Con Ops, I said to her, "So do you have gun?"

"Of course," she said. "I will travel too."

She spoke as if having a gun were normal among the fen. It wasn't. Fannish weaponry was often real—that was why conventions had a no weapons policy—but the real weapons were swords of all types, from broadswords to rapiers, and knives, usually of a decorative medieval type. Bowie knives were too Wild West for our people, except maybe here in Tahoe where the West still lingered, not just in the memories of the Donner Party, but in the toughness of the locals as well.

"You get a lot of work this way?" I asked.

She shrugged.

"I'm not trying to steal your clientele," I said. "I'm really more of a Nero Wolfe than a Sam Spade. If work comes to me, I'll do it, usually from the quiet of my computer terminal."

"You don't have orchids?" she asked.

I grinned at her. A few fen read mysteries, but not enough to know the distinction between Wolfe and Spade. That's how I got my nickname. I actually suggested folks call me Wolfe, and the people around me at the time grinned. They saw someone named Wolfe as a feral tough guy, probably a wiry man with unruly hair. They didn't realize that of all of mystery's detectives, the one I most resembled, from my wealth to my hobbies to my girth, was Nero Wolfe.

"I still like Spade, though," she said. "It's a rather gloomy pun, especially if you've worked on murders."

I had worked on everything except murders, although the case I'm most renowned for, which happened at the very first Dinocon, initially looked like a murder.

"No murders yet, thank heavens," I said. "I can't imagine what one would do to fandom."

Her lips thinned. She slipped her long fingers through the crook of my arm, sending a chill through me. She did smell faintly of jasmine, and I knew I would associate that scent with this moment for the rest of my life.

As we emerged into the large lobby, I half expected applause. It wasn't often I walked through the halls of a convention with a beautiful woman at my side. (It wasn't often that anyone did.)

I got a few thumbs up, one from a hobbit whom I recognized, another from a werewolf whom I did not recognize, and the bulk from members of the concom, recognizable by their blue tooth headphones and the walkie-talkies clipped to their jeans. Like a proper doofus, I grinned at all of them, and tried hard not to blush.

Paladin and I entered the restaurant. It was set off by a low-level shelf covered with real plants. A waitress led us to a booth near the back, surrounded by tall indoor trees. Unlike Nero Wolfe, the one place I lacked expertise was plants, so I couldn't identify anything by type—which always annoyed me. All I knew was that the plants were the normal kind you saw in restaurants, with broad green leaves and thick, well pruned branches.

We sat. I ordered a Belgian waffle since I left without having my donuts, and she ordered the FleshCon Feast off the special convention menu. I raised an eyebrow at her, deliberately Spocklike.

The FleshCon Feast had everything: waffles, French toast, pancakes, eggs, toast, and three kinds of meat. If she ate all of it, she would consume at least 5,000 calories.

I had no idea where she would put them all.

She grinned at my expression. "I have a high metabolism."

"You want to loan me some of that?" I asked.

"I could," she said with all seriousness, "but I like you just the way you are."

That flush returned, like a cough you couldn't shake. There was a thermal coffee pot on the table. I turned over one of the coffee mugs, poured myself some fresh coffee, added more cream than I usually did, and said, "So which of my expertises do you need? Computers? Convention organizing? Solving minor crimes?"

"I need your logical brain," she said. "You understand subtleties. I do not."

I thought about that for a moment. She had named herself after a character who did understand subtleties.

But the paladins that she claimed she admired, the knights errant, weren't subtle men at all. They were chivalrous adventurers, usually out to save the damsel in distress.

"I'm more of a bulldozer," she said, mistaking my silence for confusion. "I barge in, get the job done, and stomp out. That's not your reputation at all. You see things that no one else sees."

That flush deepened. I wondered if she thought that I was normally red-faced.

"What do you want me to look at?" I asked.

She slid a photograph at me. It was a picture of a young boy, maybe 13, maybe an immature 16, skinny, undeveloped, with dark hair and haunted eyes. He wore a Halo t-shirt that had been washed too many times.

There were probably ten kids who looked just like him at this convention alone, not counting the ten kids who looked like him at the twenty other conventions being held across the country this weekend.

"His name is Dyson Emmanuel," she said. "He's a runaway. His family has hired me to find him."

"His family belongs to Fandom?" I asked.

"Actually, no. He does. So they think he's traveling from con to con, surviving on food in the con suites and crashing on the floor in someone's hotel room."

Sounded pretty logical. It was a good way for a kid to stay away from home, so long as he had transportation to a convention the following weekend.

"I've been tracking him all over the West," she said. "He bums rides from convention to convention. Sometimes people put him up for the week in between. He claims he's older than he is."

"How old is he?" I asked.

"He says he's eighteen."

"What does his family say?"

"I never asked," she said. "They hired me and gave me a lead. I had to run to a small con in Sacramento. I nearly caught him there, but he slipped by me."

I was still staring at the photograph.

"Looks scrawny for eighteen," I said.

"I think he looks scrawny for sixteen," she said. "But he registers as an adult at cons."

"How does he afford that?" I asked.

"Usually he bums an extra membership off a friend. That's how I've been able to track him so far." She poured herself some of that coffee. "Plus he's moving on a rather predictable trajectory. He always goes to the con that's closest to the previous weekend's con. I tracked him here, but he's vanished, as if he knew I was looking for him."

"I can check the membership roster," I said.

"He's on the membership roster," she said. "A friend paid his fee, but in cash, so I wasn't able to track down who."

"We could look at security videos," I said. "If he eats in the con suite, we can track him. We've learned to have a camera in the con suite at all times."

The con suite was the convention hospitality suite, where the convention itself kept a spread of food and beverages. In some conventions, the con suite had only chips, fresh fruit, and soda. At other conventions, it was a true spread, sometimes purchased and refreshed by the hotel itself, featuring cold cuts, cheeses, sweets, breads—everything except hot food. And I've been to some particularly wealthy conventions—usually the large ones in places like Los Angeles and Chicago—where the con suite put out trays of hot food at lunch and dinner, as well as a full continental breakfast in the morning.

"Do you keep an hour-to-hour video record?" she asked.

"We keep footage from the entire convention," I said.

Vandalism happened at cons—no matter what we did, the concom could never prevent all of it—and sometimes we didn't find out about it until the hotel told us as we settled the final bill. By keeping video records, we usually caught the culprit, even if he had left the premises two days before.

"Well, that's a start," she said. "Normally, I wouldn't even need it, but this kid seems to have literally vanished."

"Literally?" I said dryly. Sometimes people weren't very precise when they were speaking. I felt a little disappointment in her exaggeration. I had thought she was a precise person, even though she had described herself as a bulldozer.

"Yes," she said. "I've already checked the hotel security systems, particularly all the footage they have of the various doors. The kid is inside this building. I saw video of his entrance last night. But whenever I close in on him, he's nowhere to be found."

"He's good at hiding then," I said.

"I hope so," she said. "Because I could swear I saw him disappear in front of my own eyes."

"You mean like magic?" I asked, snapping my fat fingers.

"I mean like magic," she said, making gently fun of my Valley Girl construction, a part of speech I picked up in the early 1990s and haven't been able to rid myself of since.

Then she leaned toward me.

"You have to understand something," she said softly. "I don't believe in magic."

I believed in magic, but only in the kind of magic I felt when she took my arm, the way she looked when she sat cross-legged in my chair. I believed in the kind of magic that made me hope, if only for a second, that a woman like Paladin would have a meal with me because she wanted to instead of because she needed to.

Of course, I said none of that. I hoped none of it showed on my face. I made myself focus—that legendary focus of mine, the focus that brought her to me in the first place—on the kid.

"Why did he run away from home?" I asked.

If we knew that, then we might be able to find him.

"The family doesn't know," she said. "It's the standard thing. You know, he's unhappy, he's tried it before, things like that."

"Could they pinpoint a starting point to his changed behavior?"

"Not really." She shrugged. "I get the sense that they didn't pay much attention to the kid until he ran away."

"What about his friends?" I asked.

"I couldn't find any outside of science fiction," she said.

"You mean Fandom?" I asked.

It was an important distinction. If he had science fiction friends in his hometown—other gamers, other kids he went to movies with, other readers—then we could ask them about his day-to-day activities, and what he really said about leaving home.

If all of his friends were in fandom, then they were scattered all over his local area, if not all over the country. They wouldn't see him from day to day, and they would only know him by his fannish persona—just like I only knew Paladin as Paladin, not by her birth name.

"I'm sorry," she said, apparently apologizing for not being specific. "I did mean Fandom."

I sighed heavily. That made things difficult. I couldn't tell if the difficulties came from her own admitted lack of subtlety—had she interviewed enough people about the kid?—or if it truly came from a lack of information.

As I pondered that, the food arrived. The waitress set my Belgian waffle down in front of Paladin, and then proceeded to give me the FleshCon Feast. Wait staff made that kind of mistake all the time. I was the fat guy, so I got the pile of food.

As the waitress was setting down the pile of food, Paladin shoved the Belgian waffle at me, and then grabbed the Feast plates.

"You made a mistake," she said to the waitress. "I'm the piggy eater at this table."

I've had friends say things like that with a smile, but Paladin wasn't smiling. She was admonishing the waitress for her faux pas.

The waitress had the grace to look embarrassed. "Sorry," she said, setting the remaining plates in front of Paladin. "I must have had my ticket mixed up."

"Doesn't make it right," Paladin said, stabbing her egg yolks with her fork. Yellow bled all over that plate.

The waitress hovered, uncertain what to do.

I waved my hand. "It's okay. It's a common mistake."

The waitress fled.

"You were too easy on her," Paladin said.

"And you were too harsh. Is that your normal interview method?"

"I said I'm a bulldozer," she said. "You don't hire me for delicate jobs."

She was digging into the food like she hadn't eaten in weeks. The eggs had disappeared while I was trying to deal with the waitress.

I hadn't even looked at my waffles yet.

"This job sounds like a delicate one," I said.

"No kidding," she said.

"Why did you take it?"

She paused in the act of switching the now empty egg plate with the plate of sausage, bacon, and ham. She frowned at me.

"First," she said, sounding irritated, "I didn't know it was a delicate case until I was into it. And second, I handle a lot of missing persons. I even work as a bounty hunter occasionally. That's not a job for a delicate person. Let's see you corner a felon, handcuff him, and bring him across country sometime."

I shuddered. The last thing I wanted to do was deal with the underworld. The bits of it that crept into science fiction conventions was too much for me—and those were usually white collar criminals.

"I wouldn't have brought you in," she said, shaking a half-eaten slice of overcooked bacon at me, "if I didn't need someone delicate. I got in over my head. Hence this conversation."

She had raised her voice. I had really angered her.

Then I realized what I had done. I had questioned her professional competence.

"I'm sorry," I said. "I really I am. I was just hoping for more information."

"There isn't any we can get right now," she said. "His folks are in Compton, and they don't know anything. And going back there will probably take all weekend, which would mean we'd lose the convention."

I nodded, but she didn't seem to notice, because she went on.

"I mean, I know he's here. I saw that video on security. I've tracked him this far. I just don't know how he vanishes."

"What do you mean vanish?" I asked.

"I saw him down a corridor," she said. Then she stopped and glared at me, anticipating my next question. "It *was* him. Right down to the Halo t-shirt. His hair was longer, and he was skinnier than he was in that photo—"

I had no idea how anyone could be skinnier than the kid in the photo.

"—but his face, his movements, everything told me it was him. He didn't see me, not that it would have mattered. He has no idea who I am. He walked into the con suite, so I went in there too. I saw him, right beside that pile of exotic fruit. He had picked up the whole pineapple that they'd used as decoration. Someone called my name, I turned, waved hi, and when I turned back, he was gone."

"He went out again," I said.

She shook her head. "He would have had to walk past me to get out and believe me, I would have seen that."

"So he ducked into the bathroom," I said.

"He wasn't there either. And no one else saw him, that's the weird thing. I was asking people. They had no idea some kid in a Halo t-shirt was waving a pineapple around. They would've thought I was nuts for asking, but it is an sf convention."

I grinned. She was right. At a real convention, filled with business people, the kid would have stood out. Here, he blended in with everyone else.

Then I frowned. He blended in. Some people were really good at blending in. Some—particularly teenagers of a certain type (the type that often frequented sf, comic, and gaming conventions)—were experts at blending in.

"You know roughly what time that was?" I asked.

"I know exactly," she said. "I have to keep track of time and locations for billing purposes."

I shuddered at that thought too. If you had to label me anything, you'd call me an amateur sleuth. No one pays me. I just meddle now and then.

The idea of trying to bill for my investigations made me very uncomfortable. I wouldn't know how to establish rates. Did you charge by the second for the flashes of insight? Or by the hour for the long hard work of subconscious cogitation?

I didn't ask her. Instead, I said, "As soon as we finish, we'll go back to Con Ops. I'll look up your video for you."

"Okay." She was finished. She had already stacked all five empty plates on the side of the table. For the observant focused guy I was supposed to be, I had somehow missed her eating most of her meal.

I finished my waffles quickly, paid the tab for both of us over her protests ("Microsoft Millionaire, remember?" I said when she argued), and then let her take my arm as we headed back down the corridor to Con Ops.

***

The smell of sweaty feet had oozed into the stench of unwashed bodies. Mid-convention, Con Ops. Half the volunteers had forgotten to bathe. The other half had pulled on whatever clothing they could find, whether it had been balled into a corner of their hotel room or not.

Someone had turned the overhead fan on high, but that only added a layer of burnt dust on top of the stink. The night crew had left, taking most of the donuts with them, and the day crew was scattered in front of the Towers of Terror, entering data as fast as they could.

I went to my chair. No one sat in it this time. Paladin followed me. As I sat down, she leaned against the table, half turned away from the computer screens.

At every con I'd worked since the mid-1990s, I had linked my computer with security's back-up videos. In the old days that meant I needed an extra hard drive, but modern computers had so much memory they could eat days of footage and not even burp.

I called up yesterday's footage for the floor in question, then asked Paladin exactly what time she had gone into the Con suite.

"Midnight," she said. "On the nose."

On the first night of a convention, everyone stayed awake long past midnight. The parties had started, old friends were greeting each other, and the gaming wing had just finished its set-ups.

I reversed the time-stamp on the hallway video until I found 11:50 and started from there.

"Midnight," Paladin said again, as if I hadn't believed her.

"I know," I said. "Just looking for your kid."

She frowned at me, then leaned forward. At 11:59, Paladin appeared in the video. She was wearing the same Tom Canty t-shirt and Capri pants that she wore now, proving two things to me: 1) she *had* spent the night in my chair (and that made me tingle in ways I didn't want to contemplate) and 2) she was a True Fan since she hadn't changed clothes for the first 24 hours of the convention (and she clearly didn't care).

On the video, she was striding through the corridor toward the Con suite, her head turned toward the side of the hallway.

"He's over there," she said now, touching my computer screen and leaving a buttery fingerprint on the edge. I resisted the urge to remove my handkerchief (yes, I'm old-fashioned enough to carry one) and wipe the screen off.

But I'd offended her enough for one morning.

I slowed the video down and went frame by frame, but all I caught was a blurred image on the edge of the screen. The kid was just outside camera range.

I tried using the other camera, the one mounted at the opposite end of the hallway and managed to catch the kid's back. If that was him (and I wasn't sure it was), then he *was* skinnier and his hair was longer, just like Paladin had said.

"How did he do that?" she asked. "This isn't bank security. The cameras aren't stationary or obvious."

But they were stationary and obvious to anyone who had worked a lot of conventions. There were standard places to put security cameras like, for example, above doorways at the end of major corridors, so that we could watch the attendees go in and out, or near the food in any con suite, so that we could get a good glimpse of faces.

I didn't say that to Paladin, though. She was good, but she was a bulldozer, and I didn't want all of our secrets out.

"Let's try the Con suite," I said. I switched to the Con suite's back-up vid and started it from 11:59.

It was impossible to avoid getting caught on camera when you entered a con suite. But the kid seemed to know that too. We saw him all right, but his head was down, his longish hair covering his face. I couldn't even confirm if the t-shirt he wore was the much-washed Halo t-shirt or just some generic gamer's shirt.

He hovered near the food table but didn't look at anything there either, so I only caught a glimpse of his back and his empty belt loops.

The doorcam showed Paladin as she entered, her expression tense. She looked left, mouthed "hello," and then turned her head back toward the boy. Her eyes widened and she stopped walking.

The boy had disappeared.

"See?" Paladin said to me in real time. "He's gone."

I didn't answer her. I switched to the food cams, focusing on the fruit. A scrawny hand with dirty fingernails snatched two tangerines, pocketed them, and had just grabbed a pineapple when it froze over the table itself.

His image blurred—he had been moving fast—and then he was gone.

"See?" she said. "Vanished."

I still didn't say anything, and I could tell she was getting frustrated.

Instead, I went back several frames and slowed the images down. As his hand opened to get the pineapple, the camera caught a great image of his palm.

Dirt streaks ran along the heel and his lifeline. Numbers had been scrawled in the very center. 4236.

2203. 3236. 5578. 7733. A few names had been written on his fingers. The names were all fannish monikers which would take me a while to look up.

I didn't point them out to Paladin. Instead, I let the images go by, frame by frame. His movement—which seemed blurred in real time—wasn't really blurry at all. The kid was just quick.

He must have seen the camera, and he moved away from it.

"He's still there. See?" I pointed a pudgy finger at the side of his t-shirt, which brushed the decorative lettuce leaves the hotel staff had placed under the fruit. "He just moved out of camera range."

Paladin leaned closer. She frowned at that little bit of t-shirt, and the empty belt loops. "How do you know that's him?"

So I played it for her again, showing her the detail as the kid moved from the food section to a gap in the cameras' range.

"He can't be that good," she said.

"You don't believe a member of Fandom understands camera angles, but you believe he has magical powers and can vanish on his own?"

It was her turn to blush. "I told you. I don't believe in magic. It just *seemed* like he vanished."

The day crew was listening this time. It had been years since anyone had seen the great Spade arguing with a pretty woman at a convention.

In fact, no one had seen it. This was going to be the talk of Fandom for months.

"Well, he didn't vanish," I said.

I used the door camera's imagery to show her where he was. He stood between the table and the door into the suite's bedroom. Someone had covered the wall behind the food table with a curtain—probably to dress it up—and he leaned behind that as he watched people go by.

His faded Halo t-shirt blended in with the wall's beige, and his thin frame was nearly invisible behind the curtain's folds. People walked past him without even seeing him, especially as he set the pineapple back down and grabbed two bananas, an apple, and a handful of raisins (which he promptly ate).

"He's just stocking up for the night," I said.

"I looked there," she said.

As if to prove her point, her video image did walk toward the door, but from the angle she was standing at, near the table, she probably couldn't have seen him. She was moving her head back and forth, clearly searching for someone. Then she turned away and he slipped into the suite's bedroom.

I'd been in the con suite. There was no door leading back into the hallway from the bedroom. But there was a large walk-in closet. The FleshCon's chair had laughed about it when she showed it to me, saying she planned to fill it with supplies so that no one would try to move in.

"He's just a kid who's really good at blending in," I said.

"I would have seen him," she said.

I shook my head. "You looked around, then went and looked in the bedroom and both bathrooms, right?"

"Yes," she said.

"And then you started asking people if they'd seen him."

Her entire expression froze. "He figured out who I was."

"No," I said. "He figured out that someone was searching for him, and he's going to avoid anyone he doesn't know who seems to know who he is."

"Because he's done something wrong?"

"Maybe," I said. "Or maybe because he's running away and scared."

Those dirty fingernails haunted me, and so did the snatching of food. He was hungry. He wasn't having as much luck finding places to stay as he had when he first left home.

"Well, we know what happened last night," she said. "But he could be anywhere by now."

"I doubt that," I said.

She frowned at me. "You think he's still at the con? Even though he knows I'm looking for him?"

"He'll avoid you. And he'll stay for the free food."

"So we hang out at the Con suite and capture him when he comes back?"

"Nah," I said calmly. "I was thinking of something easier."

"Like what?" she asked.

"Like getting him out of his hotel room," I said.

"He can't afford a hotel room," she said.

"You already told me that he bunks with friends," I said.

"Yeah, but I don't know who his friends are. Do you?"

Those last two words were sarcastic. And the sarcasm, as misguided as it was, pleased me.

It meant she was going to be surprised.

"I know where they're staying," I said.

She frowned. "Where?"

"Come with me, and I'll show you," I said.

***

As we walked to the service elevator, I grabbed two people off our security team and made them accompany us. We could have made do with one, but I still didn't know Paladin very well and the fact that she had a gun when she traveled bothered me more than I could say.

So when I pulled the two security guards aside (both male, both younger than I was, both just as tall, and four times more muscular), I gave them the rundown, only quietly I asked one of them to keep an eye on Paladin, instead of looking for skinny little Dyson Emmanuel.

Then our cadre went to the west wing of the fifth floor.

The west wing of the fifth floor looked like a normal hotel wing. Lots of closed doors and, since it was only 10:30 in the morning (still barely past dawn in fannish circles), lots of do-not-disturb signs. Outside a few doors were room service trays, showing the remains of burgers and nachos, and other late night snacks.

Room 5578 was in the middle of the corridor, with two other doors (5576 and 5580) equidistant on either side. That meant Room 5578 was not a suite, so it only had one potential exit.

I put my guards on either side, sent Paladin to lean against door 5580 (telling her in the service elevator that if the kid saw her, he'd bolt), and then I knocked.

"Security," I said in my deepest voice.

Paladin looked panicked. She waved a hand, trying to convince me with very bad sign language that I had made an awful choice.

I hadn't. I wanted to alarm the people inside the room.

No one answered, but I heard rustling. On the fifth floor of any hotel, especially one this new, the windows did not open. Still, I imagined the kid trying to get out that way and failing.

I knocked again. "Security. Open up or I will open the door myself."

Not that I could. I hadn't even checked with the hotel before coming up here. Privacy laws prevented them from giving me the names of the legal occupants, and I had no real knowledge of any kind of crime or terrible activity that would allow me to involve them.

So I was going it alone.

I heard more rustling behind the door. Then the door opened as far as the privacy slide would let it.

A twenty-something girl with the remains of glitter make-up and three cat whiskers still glued to one cheek peered at me.

"What?" she asked.

"Reports have come in from all over the floor of an illegal party. I need to inspect the premises. If we find you're serving alcohol in here, we will have to ask you to leave."

"We aren't," she said and tried to close the door.

I put my hand on it, and pushed just enough. "If you aren't holding a party, then you have nothing to hide. I just need to do a walk-through to placate my dark masters."

"You're not with the hotel," she said.

"That's right," I said. "I'm with the concom. You want me to get hotel security? Because if they see any damage or any hints of damage, they'll add a hefty fine to your hotel bill."

"We haven't damaged anything," she said.

"Okay," I said in that unreasonable tone that actually meant *do what you want, idiot. But you'll pay for it.* "Of course, it'll be your word against theirs. And hotels love getting more revenue from con-goers."

Someone said something softly behind her. She glanced over her shoulder, then back at me.

"Just a walk-through?" she asked.

"Just a walk-through," I repeated.

She closed the door, disengaged the security bolt and pulled the door open.

The hotel room smelled of shampoo, stage make-up, and coffee. A thin young man sat at the only table, eating a piece of cold pizza, while another girl—also twenty something—was hovering over the hotel-supplied drip coffee maker.

The two beds had been slept in, and one had an extra pile of blankets on top, with a pillow in the middle. A cat costume was hanging over one of the chairs, and another cat costume hung from the open bathroom door.

I walked in, glanced longingly at the pizza, and then wandered around as if I were inspecting.

"See?" the girl who answered the door said. "No party here."

I peered in the bathroom, saw more make-up, and some very long claw-like fake-fingernails still in their case.

"Hall costume or masquerade?" I asked. The masquerade was tonight, and some participants got very serious about it.

"Masquerade," the girl who answered the door said.

"You doing a number from *Cats* or is this something more elaborate?"

"Midnight Louie," the other girl said grumpily.

"Wow," I said. "Mystery fans. I adore Carole Nelson Douglas."

"Really?" the girl who answered the door looked at me. "You think we have a chance? It's not really fantasy."

"Talking cats aren't fantasy?" I asked.

"He doesn't exactly talk," the boy at the table said. "He just thinks a lot."

"Don't we all?" I said, as I pulled open the double mirrored doors leading into the closet. I didn't see anyone inside, but I didn't expect to.

Instead, I reached around the ironing board hanging on the wall, and grabbed an arm.

I pulled, and Dyson Emmanuel stumbled out. Up close, his Halo t-shirt looked threadbare, but he smelled pleasantly of the hotel soap. Someone, at least, had let him use (ordered him to use?) the shower.

"Well, well, well," I said. "What have we here?"

"Lemme go," he said.

"Sure." I let go.

He stumbled backwards.

"You do know your parents are looking for you," I said.

"No, they're not," he said.

"They hired my friend Paladin to find you," I said. Then I raised my voice. "Paladin!"

She hurried into the room, followed by her personal security guard. The other one remained in the hall in case the kid managed to get past all of us.

"You caught him," she said.

I shrugged a shoulder. I didn't turn around and look at her. "Tell him who hired you."

"Your family," she said to the kid.

Her construction caught me. She had been saying family all along. Not parents. Family.

He was staring at her. "Like hell."

"They did," she said, and was going to continue, but I held up one hand.

"They just want to know you're all right." I reached into my pocket and grabbed my cell phone. "Call them. Tell them you're fine. That's all they need."

His eyes filled with tears, but he didn't reach for the phone.

"Spade…" Paladin hissed at me. But I ignored her. I knew what she was going to say. The family had hired her to bring the kid back, not to have him call.

"They're worried," I said. "Call them."

The kid shook his head.

"You don't have to go back," I said. "And if you use my phone, they won't be able to find out where you are."

He stared at the phone.

"You can keep traveling," I said. "It's fun, isn't it? Never the same place week to week."

His gaze met mine. His eyelashes were wet.

"Of course," I said, "there are lots of dangers on the road. You almost didn't make it here, did you?"

His lips thinned.

"You had to jump from that last car, didn't you?" I asked.

He looked at me, startled. In fact, everyone was staring at me now. I could feel Paladin's stare, boring into my back.

"You probably should get someone to look at your hands," I said. "That dirt's embedded pretty deep."

His eyes narrowed. "How'd you know?"

"We keep cameras by the food in the con suite," I said. "I got a good view of your palm. Took me a while, but I finally figured out why the dirt bothered me so much. You'd written over it."

He rubbed his right hand on his pants.

"It's okay," I said. "I expect the room numbers vanished in your shower. But the dirt's still there, isn't it?"

He clenched his right hand into a fist.

"And you probably have scraped knees, maybe a scraped elbow or two. Is it really that bad at home? I know your stepfather is a prick, but he isn't as bad as the guy in the car, is he?"

The stepfather line was a guess, but it was an educated one, based on the word "family," not on the word "parents." And the guess seemed to hit home.

"He hates me," the kid said.

"He yells a lot," I said.

The kid nodded.

"He wants you to stop playing games, stop hanging out with your friends, maybe go out for a sport or two, something a skinny kid like you could handle, like cross-country."

"He told you?" the kid asked.

I shook my head. "I never talked to him. But he was the one who put up the money to find you." (I hoped. I couldn't turn to Paladin for confirmation.) "And he never, ever told Paladin that you were his stepson."

"He said you were his son." She stepped up beside me, understanding what I was doing now.

I felt a small thread of relief. I had guessed right.

"He's worried," Paladin was saying. "Your mom is beside herself. Take up Spade's offer. Call them."

The kid stared at the phone.

"Has he ever hit you?" I asked.

The kid shook his head.

"Physically harmed you?"

The kid's lip trembled. "He wants me to be some-one else."

"Because he wants you to put on some muscle," I said.

The kid nodded.

"So that you can fight back when the other guys at school pick on you," I said.

This time, a tear did fall. "He said it was my fault. He said if I was just normal, they'd leave me alone."

How many times had I heard that one? How many of us had become fen because we knew we would never ever be normal?

"Bill Gates wasn't normal," I said. "Steven Spielberg wasn't normal. I'll bet they got picked on in school too."

"I know they did," one of the girls said.

"It'd be great to stay here," I said, "but here only lasts the weekend. Then you're on your own. And people in the real world can be a lot meaner—a lot scarier—than the kids at school."

He nodded, probably thinking of that last car ride.

I pushed my phone toward him. He took it and punched a few numbers into the keypad.

I could hear the ringing. Then a woman answered.

"Mom?" he said, and his voice broke. "Mommy?"

He slipped into the closet and rather than go after him, I pulled the double doors closed.

I could see Paladin in the mirrors. She was staring at me.

I moved away from the closet to give the kid some privacy. "His folks'll be here either late tonight or tomorrow. If I were you, I'd wait with him, so that you get your check."

She crossed her arms. "How did you know all of this?"

"The room's easy," I said. "He wrote it on his palm."

"But there were a dozen numbers on his hand," she said.

"All room numbers, all in the party wing, except this one."

"And the family stuff?" she asked.

I shrugged again. "That's what you hired me for. The little details."

The recognizable details. My stepfather had wanted me in sports for the opposite reason. *You're already chubby*, he said. *You lose some of that baby fat and you can play basketball. You don't need to make models in the basement while you watch monster movies. It's not normal.*

"You're scary good, Spade," Paladin said.

"Nah," I said. "I just know my people."

The closet door slid open. The kid came out, his face blotchy, eyes red, but empty of tears. He handed me the phone.

"You can keep it for the weekend if you want," I said.

He looked at it as if I had offered him a million dollars. "It's your phone."

"I have others," I said.

He almost took it, then stopped. "It's okay."

"You can call them again if you want," I said.

He shook his head. "They're coming to get me. They'll be here tonight."

He directed that last at the two girls and the guy who still sat at the table.

"Then you won't be at the masquerade," said the girl who opened the door. She sounded disappointed.

"Yes, I will," he said. "If they get here early, they can watch."

The beginnings of a truce, only neither part of the family knew it yet. I handed the kid my phone.

"In case they call back," I said. "They have a way to reach you."

"I can't keep this," he said.

"Then leave it at the front desk when you go," I said. "For Spade."

"You're Spade?" he asked.

I nodded.

"Okay," he said, and closed his injured hand around the phone. "Thanks."

"No problem." Then I took Paladin's arm and hustled her out of the room. The security guard followed.

Paladin didn't dig in her heels, which I expected her to do, but when the door closed, she turned on me.

"Great," she said. "Stick by him, you said. Make sure you get your money tonight, you said. Then you leave. The kid could run off. I'm never getting paid."

I hurried her down the hall, so her voice didn't echo. When we reached the service elevator, I said, "My phone is linked to my computer. I can track it in real time. You'll know where he is. Just meet up with him at the masquerade."

"Your phone is linked to your computer?" she asked. "Why would you do that?"

"Because I can," I said. I didn't tell her the real reason: I lost my phone more times than I wanted to count. Tracking it through its GPS had saved me from buying a new phone after each and every convention.

She shook her head. "Someday are you going to tell me what made you know how that kid wanted to go home?"

"That's easy," I said. "He teared up when I told him his folks wanted to hear from him. He thought they didn't care. If he'd thrown the phone at me, we would have had a different conversation."

"He was that lonely?" she asked.

"He's that scared," I said. "And that young. I don't think he's much older than fourteen. It won't be peaches and cream when he goes home, but he knows now it's better than the road."

The service elevator stopped and the doors opened. All four of us got out. The security guards checked to make sure we no longer needed them, then headed down the hall.

Paladin didn't move.

"We should team up, Spade," she said.

I shook my head. "I don't believe in guns," I said. "And I won't travel."

"You travel every weekend," she said.

"To a convention, where I see the people I like."

"But you're good at figuring things out," she said.

"Yep," I said. "And I figured out a long time ago where I belong."

I extended my hand. She stared at it.

"See you around, Paladin," I said.

"But I owe you money," she said.

I shook my head. "I was happy to help out for free."

She still hadn't taken my hand. So I let it drop. I gave her a wistful smile, nodded, and headed down the hall to Con Ops.

After a moment, she caught up with me. She had run silently through the corridor, but the scent of jasmine preceded her.

"I can make you change your mind," she said.

"No one makes me change my mind."

She grinned up at me. "I'm not no one."

"Indeed you're not," I said.

She slipped her arm in mine. "Besides, I can't let you go. You know where the kid is. I have all day to work on you."

I flushed. "I doubt," I said, wishing I had enough courage to accent the innuendo, "that all day will be long enough."

THE KARNIKOV CARD

*F*ROM THE START, I said it was a bad idea. I told the organizers of CelebCon Five that paying the exorbitant appearance fee for Dmitri Karnikov would backfire. Yes, Dmitri Karnikov had starred in the biggest science fiction films of the 1990s. He was a megasuperstar, whose mega wattage hadn't just faded, it had imploded after a series of scandals that made Mel Gibson seem like a nice well-spoken boy.

After all, why else would someone of Dmitri Karnikov's stature be willing to make an appearance at a science fiction convention?

But Fandom is what Fandom is—which is, at its heart, a collection of fans (fen, we call ourselves). We not only believe the best of our heroes, we want their signatures in our books, on our DVDs, and across our navels. Even if we have to overlook a few stink bombs to do so.

The stink bomb I was worried about wasn't a potty-mouthed movie star on a rampage. It wasn't even some wild party in which some poor fen got both deflowered and disillusioned.

I was worried that Dmitri would take our up-front fee (which was one half of last year's CelebCon revenues) and vanish without a trace. In the few years of its existence, CelebCon, held in Los Angeles, had tried to out Comic-Con Comic-Con. Comic-Con had been the go-to convention for Hollywood types, comic book aficionados, gamers, and random sf people. It had become so big that every single hotel room in San Diego sold out a year in advance—and so did most of the cheaper hotel rooms in Los Angeles.

Deals got brokered, movies got sold, and a lot of professional writers/artists/creative types got rich on that very weekend.

CelebCon, held in March, was attracting the same kind of numbers that Comic-Con had had during its growth spurt, and there was talk—a lot of talk—that it would be the next Big Thing in entertainment.

If Dmitri Karnikov stiffed us, we'd be out more than his appearance fee. Our reputation as the upcoming Comic-Con upstart would vanish, and we'd be the laughingstock of Fandom for a generation to come.

No one in CelebCon's concom (convention committee) cared that we could lose our rep. They didn't believe that folks would laugh at us, and they figured the fen would return even after a disastrous year. This concom had no real money people, so they didn't understand that the loss of so much revenue would put the convention into a hole that it couldn't recover from.

So they went ahead against my wishes, and booked Dmitri Karnikov.

I stayed on, not because I had any loyalty to CelebCon, but because I wanted to be around for the I-told-you-so. There were a few folks who really needed to hear it, and they were going to hear it from me.

Only when the time came, I couldn't go through with it.

Because I hadn't told them so—at least, not about this.

***

Most of the time, I enjoy the respect I get from Fandom. Everyone calls me Spade. Hardly anyone knows my real name any more, primarily because I don't use it.

The nickname comes from my detecting ability. Ever since the mid-1990s, I've solved all kinds of minor (and not-so-minor) mysteries at science fiction conventions. After I solved the first one, some wag called me Spade, for Sam Spade, and the moniker stuck.

I didn't have the heart to tell the guy that the better handle would've been Nero Wolfe. I'm six-six, four hundred pounds, and set in my ways. I don't have orchids or an Archie Goodwin, but I do possess a sharp eye for detail and a critical understanding of the dark side of human nature.

So Spade it is. And in the way of the fannish, my success has become my downfall. So many young fen want to spar with me, trying to prove they've gotten the best of the Great Spade.

I don't joust very often, and when I do, the battle is verbal. The young fen have no hope of besting me in the verbal arena, just like I have no hope of besting them in the physical one. Occasionally they take a vote, like this concom did in the Karnikov matter. They thought that outvoting me was like taking me down in battle.

But the battle hadn't even begun.

***

This year's con shaped up badly from the start. We lost our venue two months in, and had to book another place with only eighteen months notice—which, for a convention of this size, was quite literally the last minute.

We sent payment to Dmitri Karnikov, locking him in as the celebrity guest of honor, and two dozen of our most beloved celebrity guests quit in protest. Some of us wanted to cancel Karnikov right there, but the bulk of the concom balked. They pointed out that preregistration was off the charts—in fact, we'd sold out the new venue five hours after announcing Karnikov—so they really didn't care that a lot of our old faithful celeb friends weren't coming. Clearly, the concom wasn't thinking of next year. Next year, when the two dozen faithful refused to be associated with CelebCon. Next year, when CelebCon would need— and wouldn't be able to get—a guest of equal drawing power to Karnikov.

However, it was my job to worry about this year's disasters, not next year's. And I was involved in a few disasters in other parts of the country, so I didn't really notice how CelebCon was shaping up.

I'm what's known in fannish circles as a Secret Master of Fandom. There's an entire group of us. We run conventions, especially the big ones. We make certain the small ones get off the ground.

We protect Fandom. I don't know about my fellow SMoFs, but I see my job this way: I keep conventions safe. I want young fen to feel like I felt when I started in Fandom. I want them to feel like they belong, like nothing bad can ever happen to them at a fannish gathering no matter where it is.

But I don't run security at conventions. I'm the Lord of Finance. My trusty computers and I manage the money for the biggest events of the year—and I teach a lot of the smaller events how to set up their financial system. Annually I run the finances for about 20 different conventions. I'm never home, and I stop answering my cell whenever a concom implodes—which is about one out of every ten. I figure the locals can work it out for themselves.

This is a long way of saying that after the preliminary planning meetings and the one emergency session about the lost venue, CelebCon wasn't really on my radar.

Until I arrived two weeks before the convention and found a disaster on my hands.

***

The big problem was that Dmitri Karnikov wanted more money. He demanded we renegotiate his contract or he'd bail out of the convention.

I did a little web surfing, found out he had just settled a multimillion dollar lawsuit with a major Hollywood studio, and it was going to cost him a wad of cash (although not as much as the studio initially sued him for).

He wanted a lot more money from us, but it didn't appear that he had another group of idiots who wanted to outbid us for him that same weekend. So if we canceled his contract (claiming we were going to renegotiate it), *he* had to pay us back three-quarters of his upfront appearance fee—since appearance is based on, you guessed it, appearing.

But the concom wasn't savvy to the ways of business and panicked when I mentioned canceling his contract altogether. Then when I said it would be a good negotiating ploy, they hit the ceiling.

The fans of Dmitri Karnikov did not want to piss off His Greatness. In fact, they wanted to offer him more money just so that he wouldn't skip out on them.

At that point, I thought I could head off disaster. The only disaster I saw was continued extortion by the unnecessarily impoverished Dmitri Karnikov.

I volunteered to negotiate with him to make sure that he would honor his contract.

The concom made me swear that I wouldn't cancel his contract, and I swore I wouldn't unless there was already a new deal in place. Of course, I didn't tell the concom that the new deal wouldn't be in writing. Cash-starved Karnikov would bend to my will or I didn't know my overspending celebrities.

The concom gave me permission to speak for them with Karnikov, and I had my people contact his people for a meet.

I'm no slouch in the negotiations department, nor am I some starstruck impoverished fan willing to do anything for my idol.

So I had no illusions as I headed to Karnikov's. I knew that I'd find dozens of hangers-on, yes-men, and so-called security guards, and I did. I also knew I'd find an out-of-control star who hadn't had someone set limits with him in thirty years.

Karnikov had a rental in Malibu although I hesitate calling anything that goes for 100K per month a rental. To me, that's like calling the Taj Mahal a McMansion. But he had to rent because most of his properties got seized in one lawsuit or another. The rest were sold off for quick cash.

As I drove through the windy roads to Malibu, I reflected on that. And my involvement with this concom. They were dumb enough to make an agreement with a man being sued by half the planet, and that was just the half of the planet who could afford lawyers. The other half would probably sue him as well, if only they could pony up the initial court costs.

I had a rental too—a high end Lexus SUV befitting my bulk. Unlike Dmitri Karnikov, I'm good with money, which is a bit like saying Superman is good at flying. Decades ago, when Microsoft was an upstart company no one had ever heard of, the illustrious Bill Gates decided to give his employees the option of being paid with cash or in company stock. I took the stock, making me a thing still known in the Pacific Northwest as a Microsoft Millionaire.

So many Microsoft Millionaires handled their money like Dmitri Karnikov handled his that there aren't many of us left. Most who remain don't work for a living, but they're not really wealthy either. Only a select few of us translated our millions into more millions.

I don't talk about money much, except to acknowledge that I have some, but there's a reason I handle the finances for more than 20 science fiction conventions nationwide.

I know what the hell I'm doing.

And Dmitri Karnikov didn't. His handlers probably did, but his handlers wouldn't get the last word. He would.

Which was why I wasn't even nervous going into this meeting. Not as I used the GPS to take me along the goat paths up the hills overlooking the ocean, not as I turned on the driveway deliberately graveled to look as if it led nowhere, not as I passed through the giant stone gate with the prominent security signs and the poor schlub manning the gatehouse who actually had to check me in as if I were entering a studio lot.

I didn't get nervous until I walked up the marble stairway leading to the marble entry designed to impress with its breathtaking waste. At the moment, I wondered what the hell I was doing, representing a concom willing to give in to a man who wasn't willing to negotiate.

Then I squared my shoulders, tucked my CelebCon One t-shirt into my good black jeans, and followed the majordomo who led me into the deliberately stunning living room.

Even a man determined not to be impressed had to pause to look at the view. The floor-to-ceiling glass walls extended over the beach, making you feel like you were floating over the ocean itself. The Pacific was its usual beautiful blue, made even more beautiful by the matching blue sky. Usually the smog extended all the way out here, but on this afternoon, the air was so clear that everything had the razor sharp edges you usually saw only in photographs.

I had to remind myself not to gape, but by then it was too late. I was gaping, and someone was talking to me.

That someone was Dmitri Karnikov himself.

I hadn't expected that either. I had expected some lawyer or financial minion or bouncer to deal with me— at least initially.

But Dmitri Karnikov was standing just past the blazing white grand piano, a clear drink in one hand and an apple in the other.

"Stunning, huh?" he asked.

The voice sounded out of place in this room. It was a famous voice, a familiar voice, one that belonged in the darkness of a movie theater or narrating some high-end car commercial on my television. I had experienced this dislocation before with other celebrities, and I never ever got used to it.

"One of the most beautiful I've seen," I said as I turned toward him.

As usual, I dwarfed him. I dwarf most people, but I dwarf actors most of all. Male actors are generally short—dunno why, just a fact that I didn't believe when I first read about it in one of screenwriter William Goldman's books. Goldman, who is tall, has made a game out of discovering an actor's real height, since most of these guys wear lifts (even, Goldman claims, in their socks).

But Karnikov was barefoot—so no lifts. He wore shorts and a Spider-Man t-shirt depicting the comic book Spider-Man, not the Toby McGuire movie version of Spider-Man.

And it was the damn t-shirt, along with the bare feet, that also threw me.

I had never considered the idea that Dmitri Karnikov wanted to come to CelebCon because he was a fan. Actors, writers, artists and other celeb types will often finagle invites to various events not because they need the face time but because they're a fan of someone attending or of the event itself.

Which meant I had forgotten one of my own rules: at heart, every single American is a member of Fandom. Most of them just don't know it yet.

I recovered enough to surreptitiously wipe my palm on my jeans before extending my hand.

"Mr. Karnikov, it's an honor—"

"Cut the crap," he said. "You're here to talk about the money."

He sounded sour. I didn't exactly blame him. No one likes to talk money, especially when they know they're being unreasonable.

"I'm afraid so, sir," I said. "Although it *is* an honor—"

"Yadda yadda yadda," he said, waving a hand as he used the outdated *Seinfeld* reference. "Can you pay the extra or not?"

"No, sir." I didn't add anything else. I didn't make excuses; I didn't remind him about the already existing contract.

I already knew I had the upper hand. Why? Because there were no handlers here. Either they'd been fired, let go because of financial reasons, or they weren't willing to make this argument for their very famous employer.

"Damn," he said, "you were my only hope."

The wistfulness with which he said that line made it a veiled *Star Wars* reference, echoing the holographic Princess Lea's line in the original movie, *Obi wan Kenobi, you are my only hope.*

I studied Karnikov for a moment. His thick blond hair was mussed and he had a bit of peanut butter on the collar of his t-shirt. He wasn't looking at me; he was looking at my reflection in the window.

In that moment, I gained some respect for him. The bare feet, the t-shirt, the *Seinfeld* reference followed by the *Star Wars* reference—he was playing me, and doing it in a very sophisticated way.

He wanted me to think we had common interests, that we were both fans, putting me at ease and giving him the upper hand. And that was why he was doing this alone.

It's easier to manipulate someone one on one.

It might have worked too, if I were ten years younger and twenty years less jaded. Or maybe if I had been a

True Fan in the first place (meaning someone who really, really, really was a fan, not just someone who liked Karnikov's work).

But I wasn't a True Fan and I was pretty damn jaded.

"Sorry," I said. "We just don't have the extra funds. But we will pay you the second half of your appearance fee by direct deposit right after your final panel, if you like. That's less than two weeks away, and the money will be instantly liquid."

I had checked our books before I arrived and saw that we could pull off the direct deposit thing—barely.

He looked at me sideways and for a moment, I saw the actor unmasked. There was avarice in those cobalt blue eyes. That was the one thing that put famous actors at a disadvantage. We had already seen every single expression they had on screen and knew how to read their faces as clearly as if they were a member of our family.

That look of avarice lasted only a half second, but that was a quarter second too long. He covered it quickly, but not quickly enough.

I had him.

"You can?" he asked.

I nodded.

"Can you do it now?" he asked.

"I'm sorry," I said. "We won't be getting the last of our money until the convention starts."

"I thought the thing was sold out," he said.

Thing. No fan would call CelebCon a thing. It would be the con or CelebCon or the convention. But never ever "the thing." Thing was what other people called our tribal meeting places. Thing bordered on a term of disrespect.

That one word was as revealing as the look, but I got a hunch he really didn't care.

"It is sold out," I said, irritated he had caught me in the lie. So I made up another one. "But we only take deposits. We collect the rest when the attendees show up."

"Stupid way to run a show," he said.

I shrugged, pretending a nonchalance I didn't feel. "That way we keep the deposits of the no-shows and sell expensive at-the-door tickets."

It sounded believable to me, and apparently to him as well. Which also proved he wasn't a fan. He would have known that prereg people not only paid in full, they got a discount for signing up early—something I would have argued about changing had I known we were going to sell out at prereg prices five hours after we announced Karnikov's presence.

"When's my last panel, as you call it?" he asked.

I was prepared for that too. "Sunday morning."

"Sunday...morning?" he asked, as if I had told him I was going to dip him in chocolate and sell the licking rights to the highest bidder. "I don't do mornings."

"You had no restrictions in your contract," I said.

"*And*," he said, "you can't transfer funds on Sunday."

"I know," I said. "But the money will be in your account and available first thing Monday morning."

He made a face. "How about we blow off Sunday? When's my last appearance then?"

"Saturday night," I said, trying not to smile. He had come prepared to negotiate. So had I. I had asked programming to tentatively schedule him Sunday morning, with the idea that we could cut that panel. If we got him to do it, fine. If not, it was a bargaining chip—a chip that was working now.

"I'll have the money Monday morning when banks open?"

"Yes," I said.

"You can't do better than that?" he asked.

"No, sir, I'm sorry."

"What about charging for autographs?"

"We pointedly advertise that we don't let anyone charge for autographs.'"

"Change that," he said.

"No," I said. "It's also in your contract. It's a deal breaker."

He crossed his arms and frowned. His eyes met mine. I recognized that look too—the look of Presidential steely determination that he had used in at least three films.

"I don't believe in deal breakers," he said.

"I've noticed," I said. "That's why you get sued so much."

"You fat bastard," he said. "You should show a little respect."

"You first," I snapped.

He looked at me in surprise. Apparently most people didn't demand respect from him.

I continued, "I have the authority to cancel your contract altogether, and if I do that, we'll demand you repay the appearance fee in full. And we'll put the entire fiasco on tonight's news so your fans know it's not us breaking the deal."

His cheeks pinked delicately, as if the makeup department had snuck in and added just a touch of color. I saw a whole new look on his face, one he had never played in all of his films.

"You think you're important. You think that you can upset my fans," he said.

"No," I said. "I don't think I'm important. I think we have a business arrangement, and I expect you to live up to your side of the bargain. Honestly, all you have to do is sit on two one-hour panels, and give a speech you've probably given 100 times before on Saturday night. You have to sign a few autographs, wave politely, and then vanish in your limo. For that, you'll make more than most people make in an entire lifetime. You don't do it, no skin off my nose."

"Your convention will collapse," he said.

Probably. But I didn't care. And that I-don't-care attitude showed in my shrug. "We had four CelebCons without you. I think we can manage a fifth without you as well."

I turned and walked away, not sure if I wanted to make it out of the room before he said something or not.

"What do they call you, fat boy?" he asked.

I continued toward the door. I'd been called fat boy in school, and I hadn't answered to it then. I certainly wasn't going to answer to it now.

"*What's your name?*" he asked with more than a little desperation.

"Spade," I said, and walked through the door into that grand foyer.

"Spade what?" he asked, following me.

I had him.

"Just Spade," I said.

"Well, Spade," he said. "You guys pay for my limo and my meals and get me the hell out of there the second that I'm done talking and we have a deal."

That was already in our contractual deal, but I didn't say that. Instead, I nodded.

"Done," I said, and left.

***

Celebrity assholes always make me feel dirty. It's like a love affair gone bad. Or maybe something even worse— like you've discovered that your beloved is a gold-digger or worse, a hooker.

Even though I wasn't a True Fan of Karnikov, I had liked his movies, and I knew, as I walked to my rented Lexus, that I would always watch them now and hear his famous voice calling me fat boy

I was mad, deep down mad, not so much at him—I had read the press; I knew he was a piece of work, even for an entitled celebrity—but at me. I had volunteered to handle him. I had been prepared for his nastiness, but I had forgotten the consequences.

And the consequences struck me in my innocent fan boy self.

I thought I had calmed myself by the time I got back to the convention site. I parked as close to the building as I could get and got out of the Lexus.

I took a deep breath, hating the dryness of the LA air, hating the heat, and headed toward the building.

"Spade?"

The female voice sent a shiver down my spine.

I turned, half expecting to see nothing at all.

Instead, Paladin stood in front of me. I hadn't even seen her as I drove up, which showed just how distracted I was.

She was slight, athletic and beautiful in a way you normally didn't see in science fiction fandom. Some of the professionals—the writers, artists, actors (the pros, as we'll call them)—achieved that kind of beauty, but not the fen. Not usually.

But Paladin was a fan. She wore faded jeans and a t-shirt with one of artist David Cherry's tough females from some book cover. It showed the depth of my distraction that I couldn't immediately summon the book's title and author.

I had barely come up with the name of the artist.

Paladin was a legend in fannish circles. I'd heard of her long before I met her. I'd initially figured she was a guy with delusions of grandeur, naming himself after the Richard Boone character in the long-lost fifty-year-old *Have Gun, Will Travel* television show. I expected this fannish Paladin to be dressed in an Old West costume and to hand out business cards that said,

Have Gun, Will Travel
Wire Paladin
San Francisco

And it turned out *she* did have a card, and the only difference from the original was that it said *E-mail Paladin@ paladinsanfrancisco.com* instead of "Wire Paladin."

I didn't contact her in order to meet her. In fact, I'd never contacted her. We first met when she wanted to consult with me on one of her cases at FleshCon a few months before.

I figured (hoped) we would stay in touch, but we hadn't. Or she hadn't.

I was too scared to contact her.

Not because she was scary, but because she was female and I was attracted.

I had forgotten how small she was. More than a foot shorter than me, thin in an ethereal way—like the elves in the *Lord of the Rings* films. She was strong, but her muscles weren't her dominant feature.

Her eyes were. Big and beautiful and filled with intelligence. Although I was also partial to her ears. She was blessed with real fannish ears, small with a bit of a point on top.

"Paladin," I said, too hot, tired, and discouraged to come up with a witty greeting. The last time we'd gotten together, we'd had a witty repartee. I wasn't sure I was repartee-ready. I certainly wasn't feeling witty.

"I can't believe you're involved with this mess," she said.

My shoulders slumped. "I get involved in a lot of messes. It's part of being a SMoF."

She shook her head. "I don't mean the standard convention mess. I mean the whole Karnikov thing."

I sighed. I was going to get it from all sides. "It wasn't my idea to invite him. I opposed him being guest of honor."

"But you didn't quit when they invited him anyway."

"If I quit every convention where I disliked a guest of honor, I wouldn't work on more than five per year," I said.

It was a sign of how tired and dejected I was that I even admitted that. Usually I kept my dislike of some people in sf prodom to myself. Multimillionaire celebrities didn't have a patent on assholeness. Sometimes five-figure writers or no-figure fans could be assholes as well.

Paladin tilted her head a little, as if she were studying me. "I didn't mean to offend you."

"You could never offend me," I said, deciding truthfulness was the mode of the day.

She smiled at that. "I'm sure I could."

"I'm not going to dare you to try," I said. "I have a hunch you can achieve anything you set your mind to."

"I wish that were true," she said. "But I learned long ago that I can't do everything."

I'd learned the same thing. And I couldn't stand in the heat and dry air, feeling dejected in front of one of the most beautiful women in the world any longer.

"If that's all," I said, "I'm in desperate need of air-conditioning and an iced coffee."

"I'll buy," she said, and pulled the door open for me.

"Paladin," I said in a chiding tone. She didn't have to buy me anything. In fact, she should never buy me anything. I was the Microsoft Millionaire. She worked hard for each and every dime.

"Give a girl a break, Spade," she said. "The last time I asked you for a favor, I was going to buy breakfast and you stole the check."

"You're asking me for a favor?" I said as I walked through the open door into a frigid interior. Someone wasn't following the environmentally friendly air-conditioning rules and I was grateful.

"I'm asking you for a favor," she said. "And I want you to think hard before you say yes."

"I promise I will," I said. "So long as I can think with an iced coffee in front of me."

"Done," she said.

And in a moment, it was.

***

Paladin had found a little coffee bar inside the convention center, a bar that I hadn't even noticed. It was small, it was dark, and it was attractive, not usually things found in a convention center. It had lovely wood tables, maroon walls covered with black-and-white Ted Croner New York at Night photographs from the late 1940s, and an actual bar with a top made of polished walnut. This little place had so much class that I doubted it would be in business the next day, let alone when the convention started.

She ordered me an iced coffee and herself an iced tea. Then she bought two pieces of lemon cake, a cinnamon bun, and a gigantic chocolate chip cookie. I would have protested, except I had watched her eat once before. I had a hunch most of those calories were for her.

She brought me two tall glasses of water even though I hadn't asked for them, and stood over me while I drank one. Then she took the glass back to the coffee bar just as our order came up.

I smiled at her concern. Apparently, I looked as bad as I felt.

She rested the tray on one hand, removed the drinks first, and then the food. She waved a piece of lemon cake at me.

"You don't have to have it," she said, and I couldn't tell from her tone whether or not I would disappoint her if I ate it. Maybe she wanted it.

I took the cake. Breakfast had been a long time and one nasty celebrity ago.

She straddled the chair across from me, and picked up her fork like a weapon. Then she looked at me, as if daring me to comment on all her food.

I didn't. I took one dainty bite of the lemon cake—which was better than expected—and slurped some of the iced coffee.

By the time I'd done that, she had already eaten the cookie.

"Thanks for this," I said.

She nodded, halfway through the cinnamon roll.

"You mentioned a favor."

She nodded again, finished the cinnamon roll, and pushed the cake aside, as if she were saving it for later.

"I want to head security," she said.

"The convention center takes care of security," I said.

"For the convention itself," she said.

"We have a security director," I said. I liked the director, Doris Xavier. I trusted her. She was another SMoF. We'd worked dozens of conventions together.

"I know," Paladin said, "but I think it's better if I'm in charge."

I wasn't so certain. The last time we ate together—on our first and only case together so far—she had described herself as a bulldozer. In fact, she had asked me to work with her because she liked my finesse and thought herself incapable of the same thing.

We resolved the case—rather, I resolved the case—with that finesse.

A lot of times, convention security required a delicate touch. We were dealing with paying guests, after all, as well as some well-known people. One bulldozer moment could create a crisis that would reverberate through Fandom for years to come.

"Why don't you just tell me what's going on?" I said.

Paladin looked over her shoulder, then glared at the barista behind the counter. The woman moved to the other side of the tiny coffee bar. Paladin took her lemon cake, and cut off a piece, staring at it.

"I've been trying to get Karnikov for years," she said.

"Excuse me?" I hadn't expected that. "Get him for what?"

She stared at me as if I should know. Then she raised her eyebrows.

"Okay, I know he's an ass." I felt the reverberation of that "fat boy" comment all over again. "I know he's broken dozens of contracts, drinks too much, and is uninsurable. I know he can be violent on set. Everything the tabloids know, I know. And I have no idea why you would want to 'get' him."

"You should have a list," she said, and there was crispness in her voice I had never heard before, as if just talking about Karnikov disgusted her.

"I had a file," I said. "I made it up when the concom was considering Karnikov. I did have a list—more than 100 reasons not to book this guy. But—"

"Not that kind of list," Paladin said. "Don't you SMoFs have a list of the people to watch at conventions?"

It took me a moment to understand her, primarily because I didn't handle security. She meant The List, passed from convention to convention, of troublesome adults. Science fiction, gaming, and comic book conventions attract kids. Any place that attracts kids also attracts their predators.

Unfortunately, some of those predators were Big Name Fans and professionals in the field. The people we couldn't throw out of a convention without cause, so we didn't. We also didn't let them give us cause. We usually assigned security people to dog these troublesome adults, and to never, ever let them be alone with a child or a teenager. We also made sure these troublesome adults stayed away from the child-care areas and the places where kids went unsupervised, like the gaming wing and the movie room.

"Of course we have a list," I said. "But believe me, Karnikov isn't on it. I know. That was the first thing I checked when the concom wanted to book him. If he was on The List, I would have made sure that we had no guarantors for the hotel or the convention site."

"He should've been on The List," she said.

"He never came to a convention before," I said. "He's not on The List because he hasn't needed our tiny level of money before."

"Grow up, Spade," she said. "He's not coming here because he's broke. He's not that broke. He's got more residuals than you can imagine. He's coming because he's running out of venues where he can get his hands on kids."

My breath caught in my throat. Could she be right? How could I have missed that? "I saw no evidence of that in the press."

"You're not dumb, Spade," she said. "Why do you think the press doesn't have any of this?"

I grew cold. It was an internal coldness, not caused by my iced coffee or the air conditioning. I was appalled.

"He bought them off," I whispered.

"Or threatened suit," she said. "And those suits can get ugly, especially if the press doesn't have a lot of evidence."

"But you do," I said.

She shrugged one slender shoulder. "I would have evidence, if it weren't for his damn money."

I had finished my iced coffee, and somewhere in our conversation, she had finished her final piece of cake. I stood up.

"I'm getting more coffee. Do you want anything?"

"The entire contents of the sweets cabinet," she said, then raised a hand. "Kidding."

But she didn't sound like she was kidding, and I understood stress eating. So I bought her a piece of marble cake and got me another iced coffee. I still had my lemon cake, which I wasn't sure I could eat—at least not during this conversation.

"Okay, you've got to tell me what's really going on," I said as I slid the marble cake toward her.

She closed her eyes, took a deep breath, and said, "You're not going to like this, Spade."

"I already don't like it," I said. "I doubt anything you tell me will be worse than the things my imagination can conjure."

***

But it was. Oh, it was.

And I was very glad I hadn't eaten any of that lemon cake. Paladin ate it, along with her piece of marble cake, and two shortbread cookies that she bought when she refreshed her ice tea.

All the while, she told me things I didn't want to know and would certainly never forget.

The PG-rated version went like this:

A large part of Paladin's business came from distraught parents whose kids were missing. These parents had tried everything to find the kids—or, conversely, the parents were really famous/upscale/visible, and wanted a discreet investigator, someone below the radar to track down the missing kid.

The parents in the second category usually had runaways who were acting out, kids who had trust funds and lots of access to cash, kids who really wanted to get away from Mommy and Daddy. Paladin and I met over a case like that.

But a handful of these kids were last seen in the company of Karnikov. Initially, he met them at big celebrity events, and invited the kids to his place for an afternoon, something starstruck parents couldn't say no to. And by kids, Paladin meant prepubescent teenage boys—ten to thirteen year olds. They were all good-looking in a teen model sort of way, and they were all Karnikov fans.

Until he spent time alone with them. Then they hated him, and for good reason.

But they often couldn't leave his house. Paladin rescued two from hotel rooms, five from the house itself, and five more from limos. She prevented half a dozen kids from leaving a public venue with Karnikov.

Since a lot of these events happened in San Francisco, she got one of the district attorneys there to hold grand jury hearings on a group of cases.

The problem was that by the time it came to testify about Karnikov, the kids had either left the country or they wouldn't talk to her any more. In all of the cases, she could prove that the parents had come into a large sum of money. But she couldn't prove where the money had come from, even though she knew.

Until she could prove who was paying off the kids, the DA wouldn't press charges. And with Karnikov, it was his word against theirs.

"Wouldn't he recognize you?" I asked when she finished.

"No," she said. "He's never seen me. And he changes his security people all the time. Some of the older ones would recognize me, but the new ones have no idea who I am."

"What do you want to do?" I asked.

"I want to set up cameras all over his hotel suite. I want to bug it as well. I want images. I want to catch this bastard in the act."

She struck her clenched fist on the table, nearly knocking off the stack of dessert plates beside her. I grabbed them, got up, and handed them to the barista.

Then I came back to the table. The movement didn't help. I still felt profoundly disturbed.

"I don't want to catch him in the act," I said softly, "because that means a child gets hurt on our watch, at our convention."

At *my* convention.

"I would never allow him to touch anyone," she said so fiercely that a few people looked over at us in alarm.

"I know," I said, "but even a hint of an allegation could hurt the child involved. You know that the less scrupulous members of the press will broadcast the kid's identity. You know that they'll trash the kid and his parents in any forum they have."

Her cheeks reddened. It was a lovely color that set off her eyes.

"I hadn't thought of that," she said. "I was just thinking OJ, you know? They caught OJ in a hotel with his own words."

Former football star OJ Simpson, who later confessed to murdering his wife, got brought down by his own voice on a digital recorder, threatening a man he wanted to do business with.

It was a good model, but not good enough. People didn't hate Karnikov as much as they hated Simpson. And this time, there were minors involved.

Not to mention the reputation of all of Fandom. We have perverts and creeps, just like any gathering of adults. We probably have them in fewer numbers than most places, just because our group is so uniformly shy. And we have arranged for the arrest of several, including a former SMoF who, last I heard, was serving a decades-long sentence. Those we can't arrest, we monitor.

All the time.

But Paladin was right; Karnikov was different. He had more money than anyone who had ever been the Guest of Honor at a convention and he had more fans—the loony kind, who believed everything he did was all right, even when it wasn't.

Even if Paladin's plan occurred, and even if the kid wasn't harmed, the kid and his family would be destroyed. CelebCon would be ruined, and Fandom might never be the same.

I shook my head. "I can't let you work security, Paladin."

"Okay, Spade, at least let me go after Karnikov," she said. "This is my best chance."

"No." I used my firmest voice. "I don't even think you should come to the convention."

She looked startled, then hurt. "Spade, I can buy a damn membership if I want."

"And I can block it," I said.

"You'd protect a man like Karnikov just because he's your guest of honor?"

That hurt me, but I let it slide because I knew how angry she was.

"No," I said. "I think you're going at this like a bulldozer. And right now, what you need is a little finesse."

She paused. The anger left her face, replaced by a puzzled frown.

"What're you thinking?" she asked.

"I'm thinking you were on the right track with the district attorney," I said. "You just didn't take it far enough."

"I took it as far as I could," she said.

"But you need a forensic accountant," I said.

"A what?"

"Me," I said. "You need someone like me."

***

It took some finagling. First I had to explain to the San Francisco District Attorney that I am a certified forensic accountant in California, even though my residence is in Washington State.

Over the years, I've gotten certification in every state that offers it. I'm licensed in all but Hawaii because I've never run a convention there. I usually use my forensic accountant abilities in cases where some fan running the convention decides to embezzle from it.

I make sure I can testify in court, which means getting whatever each state needs to make me a legitimate witness.

Mostly, though, I'm so well known in the fannish community that any time a con committee hears I'm investigating their finances, they panic and tell me everything they know.

I haven't lost a case yet.

Paladin knew that Karnikov was bribing the parents of these kids he hurt. She just couldn't prove it. The District Attorney couldn't afford the money to fight and track down all of Karnikov's financial dealings.

But I could. Mostly because I could do it myself—so long as we had the proper warrants, which I left to the DA.

I had Paladin supply me with pizza, Chinese take-out, huge breakfasts, and lots of donuts, as well as coffee, iced coffee, and the occasional bottle of water (but only because she insisted).

I locked myself in my hotel room with my bank of computers and went to work.

But not before I talked to the other SMoFs. Because my actions were about to make CelebCon a disaster.

We were going to time Karnikov's arrest so that he would be in jail instead of attending CelebCon. Which meant that the convention would either have to shut down or have some kind of equivalent guest.

Which we couldn't find. Not ever, not because of the short notice, but because celebrities of Karnikov's stature—megacelebrities, the press calls them—don't go to Comic-Con, let alone to an upstart convention like CelebCon.

But the SMoFs called in every chit they had, pulling in some of the lesser celebrities who had initially left the convention, offering signing bonuses, all kinds of perks that a con never normally offered.

The idea was to salvage at least a small percentage of the attendees, so that CelebCon would at least make its nut.

And if we timed Karnikov's arrest to the very last minute, then CelebCon wouldn't be blamed for his absence—or for demanding our money back, since everything was based on his actual appearance.

But all of that meant I had to work hard and fast, and most importantly, accurately. I needed to document everything, and because we were doing this on the QT, I couldn't have help.

Which meant that I couldn't have sleep.

I got crankier and crankier as time went on, so cranky that I didn't even care if I snapped at Paladin. She was doing her best to keep me upright, hydrated, and thinking clearly.

She also, bless her, never once asked me how I was doing.

Because it was pretty clear that I was doing poorly.

Karnikov had some good money managers.

And it took me five days to realize that money managers were human—and could be bought like everyone else.

***

I sent Paladin to the manager that hadn't handled Karnikov's most recent transactions. I figured two things: Karnikov had probably fired the guy and in that circumstance, a bulldozer might be exactly what we needed.

Especially a beautiful bulldozer with a killer smile.

What I wanted from the manager seemed small enough: the names of the dummy corporations that Karnikov used or, failing that, the names of the offshore banks where he kept his accounts.

Paladin got both things, but wouldn't tell me how. She did shudder when she handed me the disk with the information. Then she took a long hot shower.

It was only later I realized that she'd bullied the guy into letting her drive him to San Francisco to make a deal with the district attorney. She said being alone with the creep in the car was more than enough to make her feel slimy.

Leave it to my prurient imagination that she had done more to get the information. I blamed my lapse on lack of sleep—and that damned attraction I had for her.

Two more days, one illegal maneuver that I would have to cover with a legitimate one before we went to court, and I finally had the information we needed.

Karnikov had indeed paid off the families. All of them.

And from the same numbered offshore account.

After a short argument ("But I can drive!" "You're in no shape to walk, let alone drive!"), Paladin drove me to San Francisco to present the evidence to the district attorney myself. I slept the whole way—and had nightmare after nightmare of Karnikov trolling the halls at CelebCon, searching for victims.

I woke up in a cold sweat, ready to nail the bastard to the wall.

***

The arrest made international news. In fact, it fed the 24-hour news cycle for weeks, and got revived every time there was a legal action. The trial had a little more dignity than I would have expected, only because it was held in San Francisco, and not in Los Angeles, home of the celebrity nutball trials.

CelebCon didn't lose as much money as I thought it would. Everyone there spent the weekend discussing Karnikov anyway. His fans needed a place to gather, and they had already paid for this one. We only gave back 5% in refunds which, considering I was expecting 75%, was pretty damn good.

My I-told-you-sos weren't nearly as satisfying as I'd hoped they'd be. Mostly because I kept thinking about how close we really had come to megadisaster.

If I hadn't stayed, then Karnikov would've preyed on kids throughout the convention.

If Paladin hadn't tried to bulldoze her way into security, we might've been facing lawsuits ourselves for fostering the wrong kind of atmosphere for children, something the fen never ever ever wanted to do.

As disasters went, this one was not nearly as bad as it could've been.

It could've been the end of the fannish world.

But it wasn't.

And, as Paladin said to me one giddy afternoon before I gave my eighty-fifth deposition (actually just my third, but it seemed like 85 at that point), we'd also taken a major predator off the streets.

"You did it," she said, clutching at my arm. "You're a genius."

I shook my head. I usually accept the genius label, but not this time. This time, I still felt like a chump who should've fought harder to keep Karnikov away from my beloved conventions.

"I'm not a genius," I said.

"Oh, but you are," she said. "You're the Elliot Ness of science fiction."

I frowned at her. I'd been called a lot of things, but never that. "How so?"

"Al Capone," she said. "They got him on tax fraud, not for all the murders and stuff. But he still went away forever."

Bribery. Buying off witnesses. Interfering with court cases. Certainly not the same league of felony as the charges of child sex abuse that Karnikov could've faced.

But, as my beautiful bulldozer pointed out, those charges were alleged anyway. Mine could be proven.

"And," she said in that same joyful tone. "We all know how well child abusers fare in prison."

We did know that. Just like we knew that meeting our idols wasn't always a great idea. They didn't all turn out as bad as Karnikov, but they rarely lived up to our ideals either.

As we went into the last day of CelebCon, I was actually thinking of no longer running conventions. I had done enough. I thought I might even take a vacation from Fandom, go live in the real world for a while.

Then I ran into Doris Xavier, the head of security, outside closing ceremonies. Doris was a muscular woman the size of the Rock, and she always spoke her mind, even if you didn't want to hear it.

"That Paladin is something," she said. "Think of all the kids she's rescued. She's risked her life dozens of times. Now, she's a true hero—and we don't even know her name. Just like the real Paladin."

I almost corrected Doris. First, there was no "real" Paladin. He was a fictional character, and we did know his name.

But Doris was right. You could look at the worst side of human nature, or you could look at the best of it.

Karnikov was the worst.

Paladin was the best.

And she came to me when she needed help. Which was better than any I-told-you-so.

It was enough to restore your faith in human nature. Or at least to restore mine.

I'm still working finances at too many conventions per year. I had to take some time out to testify. I could've become a celebrity in my own right, but I didn't think I'd be a good interview, no matter what the producers on CNBC's various money shows told me.

Instead, I've been going to panels in my spare time, participating in fannish discussions—the kind that got me into the field in the first place—and I've decided to trust my instincts.

If I think a guest is going to be bad for a convention, I'm going to make sure that guest never ever attends.

I'll play the Karnikov card.

And considering how long fannish memory is, playing it once should be more than enough.

PANDORA'S BOX

WE STOOD IN the center of the second floor lobby, staring down at the beautiful handmade box, sitting on top of another box not nearly as fine.

"Told you," Paladin said, her muscular arms crossed.

No one looked at her. No one dared.

There were six of us—two members of hotel security, two members of convention security, Paladin and me. The "told you" was for me.

"I think we should call the bomb squad," said Phil, the youngest, thinnest member of con security, so thin I had no idea how anyone could ever feel threatened by him. He was new. They were all new, even the hotel security guards, although not for the same reason.

The hotel had been finished just before the Great Recession started—maybe days, maybe weeks, maybe months before, depending on what you counted as the beginning of the recession—whether it was former Presidential candidate John McCain's declaration that the economy was "tanking" and he needed to shore it up or whether you counted it from the collapse of Lehman Brothers, or whether you counted it from the first signs in what I call the Canary States, the ones that don't have the economic base that allows them to thrive in good times, let alone survive the bad.

The hotel needed business, and CrapCon was business, although not very good business, which is why I'm calling it CrapCon instead of by its real name. I'm not even going to give you the name of the town where CrapCon was held because that would help you figure out which con it was. Even after a debacle as big as this one, I'm still protecting Fandom and science fiction conventions and all things Geek.

Protection is part of my job, although it's not in the job description. Not that I have an actual job description. By IRS standards, I'm no longer employed, choosing to manage my investments—which were nicked during the rundown into the Great Recession, but not really harmed, since unlike most people (including the so-called experts), I actually saw this thing coming—and I moved my millions with months to spare.

That's right. Millions with an "m." I'm what is still sometimes called in the Pacific Northwest a Microsoft Millionaire, being one of those early employees of Microsoft who got stock options in addition to a salary, and who divested before Microsoft became—also in Pacific Northwest parlance—the Evil Empire. I left the job with millions and unlike so many of my Microsoft Millionaire colleagues, I invested wisely, turning a small fortune into that rarity, a large fortune.

But that wasn't the job I was doing at CrapCon. At CrapCon, I was doing what I consider my real job. I'm a SMoF—a Secret Master of Fandom, fandom being, but not limited to, Science Fiction Fandom which, in my opinion, involves anyone who likes, has read, or watched sf. But true fandom, the kind I'm protecting here, involves the fen—the hardcore fans, who like to socialize with their sf heroes at places like Worldcon or Comic-Con or CelebCon. I fly across the country, setting up systems at young conventions or helping conventions like CrapCon get back on track.

Although by this point, "on track" was pretty close to "not too far off the rails." CrapCon wasn't even 24 hours old and already stinking to high heaven. The organizers hadn't even issued a programming schedule, at least one people could read, so attendees were wandering the halls, peering into conference rooms to see if there was anyone worth listening to. The program participants got a schedule, but no one else did.

And now this.

Marvin, the other member of con security, hovered over the box. He looked like he wanted to touch it, but he knew better.

We all knew better.

The hell of it was that box was one of the most beautiful things I'd ever seen. It was clearly handmade—carved out of porcelain or resin or pottery clay or glass or something. I couldn't get close enough to make a real examination. It had been painted blue, purple and gold, which wasn't as gaudy as it sounded. The hand-carved figure of a beautiful woman who looked astonishingly like Paladin (only with long flowing hair, wearing a long flowing gown that I knew—without asking—Paladin wouldn't be caught dead in) lounged on the top of the box, looking like she wanted to seduce all of us. Little boxes littered the area around her, all of them replicas of the box itself, done in miniature.

Work so fine that I hadn't seen anything like it in a Worldcon Art Show or in a Comic-Con dealers room where they have the truly, truly, truly high-end stuff.

This box was stunning and startling, and just by its very beauty, enticed you to pick it up. Which, fortunately, none of us had.

"What do we do now, Spade?" asked Marvin, the other convention security guard.

Spade isn't my real name, but it's what everyone calls me. Only a few in Fandom even know my real name and that's because they worked with me all those decades ago at Microsoft. I prefer Spade most of the time—it's fannish recognition of my peculiar talent: I can solve crimes like the great detectives of old. Most fen think I'm like Sam Spade, but I'm not that thin or that cynical. If I resemble any of the great fictional detectives of the mid-20th century, it's Nero Wolfe. I'm 6'6", four hundred pounds (give or give), and horribly overeducated. I just venture out of my brownstone a heck of a lot more often than he ever did.

"I think we should call the bomb squad," Phil repeated, his voice shaking nervously.

Paladin crouched, her slender hand reaching for the box.

"Lady, don't," one of the hotel security guards said with great panic.

First, I'd never call Paladin "lady." She's tiny and beautiful, but there the resemblance to a lady ends. She also has more muscles than all of us combined, and she has that thin Buffy-the-Vampire-Slayer kick-butt heroine thing going for her. What endears her to me, besides her toughness and her sharp tongue, are her ears, which are ever so slightly pointed, giving her an elfin look. Strap a broadsword across her back, put a knife on her hip, and add a little dirt along her chin, and she'd look like part of one of the good guys heading to Mordor in Peter Jackson's *Lord of the Rings* trilogy.

Second, Paladin knows what she's doing. She's not someone whose work you question even if it is… questionable.

"Ma'am," the security guard said louder. "I don't think you should touch that."

She leaned farther in, craning her neck so that she could see all sides of the box. "It's not a Chinese Puzzle Box," she said.

I could have told her that from my vantage up here, but I let her talk.

"It's more like one of those medieval lock boxes, although it's not really one of those either." Her hand still hovered over the box, too close for my comfort.

"Lady," the security guard said, panic so deep in his voice that it made my heart pound harder. "Please. Don't."

"I think we have to turn or depress one of those little boxes," she said.

"*Don't!*" All four security guards said in unison.

She raised her head and gave them all a withering look. "I'm the one who called this in, remember?"

"I still think we should call the cops," Phil said, this time to Paladin, showing more toughness than I expected.

"Oh, don't worry," I said. "I already did."

***

Sadly, it's not that unusual to see cops at sf conventions. Ideally the cops are off duty and carrying an armload of books. But every now and then, they've been called in by a scared member of the hotel staff or some other patron who, upon seeing a Klingon in full dress uniform, gets scared and thinks some kind of invasion is going on.

I've seen cops deal with unexpected deaths (usually a heart attack) or the occasional riot (really just overexuberant fans trying to get too close to their favorite writer or actor), but I'd never seen cops come to investigate a bomb scare.

And that's what this was, although I didn't tell the police that. If I had, they would have evacuated the hotel, which would have made CrapCon famous, along with that D.C. convention where two non-fans used a sprinkler head on the ceiling as part of their bondage party and managed to break the entire fire suppression system, getting the fen (and not those two people!) banned from that hotel chain for more than a decade.

I told the dispatch that there was a suspicious object, but this being a science fiction convention, suspicious objects were relatively common and could they bring their experts in quietly, which they promised to do.

Quietly, however, was not how the day started for me. The day had started for me on the floor of the Hospitality Suite with my cell phone vibrating against my left ear.

I had apparently passed out in the middle of a late-night discussion about Australia's growing Geek culture which, if I remember correctly, included some YouTube video of the rock group Tripod, comparing them favorably to the Bare Naked Ladies. Someone had made some Blue Goo, and I had too much of it, and the room was spinning.

CrapCon's version of the Blue Goo had neon blue dye, a lot of alcohol of varying types, and some kind of sweetening agent. I usually didn't drink like that—especially when I couldn't identify half the ingredients of the concoction, but after the day I'd had—hell, the week I'd had—I felt I deserved something. CrapCon really wasn't worth saving, although I'd given it the old college try, and I decided I'd have some fun while I went down with the ship.

That, along with Tripod's YouTube version of "Hot Girl In The Comic Shop," was the last thing I remembered.

Until the phone vibrated against my ear, and I realized that I had drooled in my sleep on a heavily trampled rug that smelled vaguely of beer and vomit. Or maybe not so vaguely.

I blinked hard to open my eyes, saw party cups, two other passed out members of the convention committee, and three random fen, all of whom looked like they too had been victims of the Blue Goo.

The Blue Goo still glowed in its gigantic punchbowl, waiting for its next victims, although the glow was a bit muted by half a layer of water from the melted ice. Either that or the vodka had separated from the rest of the ingredients, a thought that made my stomach churn.

The phone vibrated again, which made my teeth ache. I sat up, wiped the drool off my mouth and did not look at the Caller ID before picking up the line.

"What?" I said, although it sounded a lot more like "Wha…?" even to my rather forgiving ear.

"Spade?" Paladin.

I sat up. Jeez, that woman had a talent for finding me at my worst. Of course she did. She was one of the few attractive women on the planet who actually liked spending time with me, not because she was attracted to me, but because we were in the same business, kinda.

As she liked to remind me, she actually got paid for the crimes she solved. And she didn't solve them with finesse and brilliance and observation. She solved hers with her fists—and when that didn't work, she actually fought dirty.

Mostly, Paladin rescued people. She took her business card from the old *Have Gun, Will Travel* television show from fifty years ago. She wasn't Richard Boone, and she didn't offer her services from some saloon in San Francisco, but then again, this wasn't the Old West, either. Instead of asking folks to wire her like Boone's card did on the show, her business card said:

Have Gun, Will Travel
E-mail Paladin@paladinsanfrancisco.com

She got a lot of work that way. Heartbreaking, hard work, most of it, tracking runaways and child molesters. But her fannish work wasn't heartbreaking; it was the stuff of legends. I most admired her takedown of an art dealer selling fake limited editions, but the fen loved her rescue of a kidnapped Chihuahua, a famous one that had won a lot of costuming awards (don't ask). Paladin hated talking about that job, because she felt it had been beneath her.

Besides, she had solved it in less than an hour, and then the damn dog bit her.

"Spade?" she said again, this time sounding worried.

"Yeah," I said and ran a hand over my face. "Yeah, it's me."

"It doesn't sound like you."

I shrugged, which she couldn't see, and said, "Yeah, well, you woke me up."

"I thought the Great Spade didn't sleep at cons."

I usually didn't, but those were cons that I enjoyed. "Not sure if I actually fell asleep."

"Then how could I have—oh, never mind," she said. "I'm in Con Ops. Your chair is here, but you're not. Nor are you in your room. So where the hell are you?"

"How do you know I'm not in my room?" I asked, still rubbing my hand over my face.

There was a long silence on the other end. She probably didn't want to tell me how she could get into the room even though she didn't have an official keycard, and I didn't want to tell her how thrilling and appalling it was to think of her in my room, running her beautiful hand across the undisturbed bed while she thought of me.

That thought made me press my fingers on the furrow in my forehead. I'd learned long ago about the futility of thinking about beautiful women in connection to me. I just tended to forget while hung over on Blue Goo.

"What are you doing here?" I asked. Last I heard, she was working a case in Nevada. Which, as you can now guess, was not where CrapCon was held.

"Looking for you," she snapped. "I need your help."

When Paladin needed my help, my heart soared. It meant I got to spend time with her. It also made me nervous and self-conscious.

"Get down here," she said. "This can't wait."

"It'll have to," I said. "I need fifteen minutes."

I needed three days. I'd slept in my clothes and someone else had clearly slept on them. Or walked on them. Then there was the matter of the Blue Goo sweat stink and the drool marks. I wasn't about to let Paladin— or anyone, really—see me like this.

"I'm coming up to your room, then," she said.

"No, you're not," I said. "I'll be down in fifteen minutes. Get donuts. And coffee. I'll need coffee."

"We don't have time—"

I hung up on her. I'd never hung up on Paladin before, but I hung up on her now, because I had less than fifteen minutes to shower and shave and find clean clothes. If I took my full fifteen minutes, she would have barged into my room, which would have created a memory I wouldn't have been able to handle.

I hurried—and I'm not the kind of man who hurried, and wouldn't have been even if I had the build for hurrying. Fortunately, my room was only one floor up and the staircase wasn't far.

I found an unworn and supposedly slimming black t-shirt that had "Evil Genius" emblazoned in red across the center, and a pair of black pants that I had only worn once (I think). I showered slower than planned (damn Blue Goo hangover) and shaved so fast that I shocked myself.

I still managed to get down to Con Ops with two minutes to spare.

Paladin was sitting in my chair, munching on a Krispy Kreme. My chair is huge, form fitting, and extremely expensive. I have it—or one of its five cousins—shipped to whatever convention I'm working on that weekend, along with my Tower of Terror, the computer system that is constantly being upgraded and moved from one convention to another.

Paladin had her back to the Tower of Terror. She sat cross-legged in my chair, managing to look like a small but powerful child-ruler of a small but formidable foreign country. Or she would have, if she didn't have powdered sugar on the tip of her nose.

"What's this emergency?" I said grumpily. Not that I was feeling grumpy (despite the remnants of the hangover). I never felt grumpy when I saw Paladin. But I'd found that grumpy was a great defense with beautiful women because that way they'd never know how pleased I was to see them. Pleased never got me anywhere. Grumpy always got me a normal conversation and a good friendship.

She eased herself up slightly and reached into her back pocket, pulling out a folded piece of paper. She handed it to me.

I took my own Krispy Kreme as I unfolded the e-mail. I munched as I read.

It was an e-mail from her paladinsanfrancisco account. The subject header was "Pandora's Box."

The body of the e-mail read:

> *The Evils have already Flown. I leave you this one Hope in the form of a warning:*

> *Today's Bomb, which I will Place in the ___ Hotel in your honor, will be a small one.*

"Good Lord," I said. "Did you call the cops?"

"What was I supposed to say?" she asked. "I got an e-mail bomb threat for CrapCon? They'd think I was threatening the convention. Have you ever seen what cops do when they think you're issuing a bomb threat?"

I hadn't. I didn't want to. "It sounds like you have."

"They want to solve things easily. Ergo, the person who mentions the threat is the person who issued the threat."

I liked the "ergo," but I didn't say so. I just gave her a rueful smile. "So this has happened to you before."

"*Spade!*" she snapped. "Focus."

I blinked and grabbed another Krispy Kreme. My first seemed to have disappeared. Then I took the coffee that she had brought for me and put it into the ancient microwave OPs kept near the back of the room. If anything was going to explode, it would be that old machine.

"I took the liberty of scanning security footage while I was waiting for you," she said. "And before you ask, I arrived with the damn Krispy Kremes. I didn't see anything."

"In the security footage," I said.

"Anywhere," she said.

"And, I take it, you have no idea who sent this e-mail."

"The URL is spoofed," she said. "I tracked the real URL through three countries. Whoever it is, they know what they're doing."

"You don't have any idea who it is?"

Usually, if someone went to the trouble of threatening me, I had an idea who they were.

"No," she said a bit too curtly.

"I didn't see your name on the guest list," I said. "How did they know you'd be here?"

"I wasn't supposed to be here," she said.

"Then why target this hotel this weekend?"

"Probably because they knew you'd be here," she said.

I stared at her. The question on the tip of my tongue was *Why should that matter?* But I couldn't quite bring myself to ask it, in case the answer was, *Jesus, Spade, it's a* science fiction convention. *Fen would die.* Without—of course—any mention of me.

"Well," I said, trying to sound calm, "that narrows the possibilities to someone in fandom."

"Or someone newly on the outs with fandom," she said.

"Or someone with a longtime grudge against fandom," I said.

"Or someone who hates fandom," she said.

"Or someone with a grudge against you," I said.

"But it doesn't matter who," she said. "Not if they're serious. We have to find this thing and get it out of the hotel."

"It might not be that simple," I said. Bombs weren't always carryable. "Let's find it first, then decide what to do with it."

She bit her lower lip, then sighed. I frowned. She hadn't moved out of my chair. Was she frightened? I'd never actually seen Paladin frightened before.

"What's this really about?" I asked her softly.

"I don't know," she said.

"But you have an idea," I said.

"*I don't know*," she repeated in a do-not-ask-me-again voice.

"I'm going to contact hotel security and con security. We need eyes on this thing. You need to check the children's areas now. Day care's not open yet. If this is a real whack-job and not some fan with a grudge, they're going to go for the soft target."

Paladin's mouth opened slightly. Then she hustled out of the chair and launched herself across Con Ops. I'd never seen her move so fast.

That scared me.

So I called the cops.

***

I didn't say we had a bomb threat. I didn't use the word "bomb" at all. I said that we had a delicate situation, one that required finesse, that we had two thousand guests at our convention, and if they got wind of this, they'd panic. I said we needed someone who was of rather high rank in the police department, not just beat cops, but someone who could make a decision quickly, and I needed that person to get in touch with me, and me alone, when they got to the hotel.

Then I gave them my cell number, the hotel's security line, the convention security line, and told them that I'm Spade. No one asked my real name. No one even asked for my first name.

But they did take me seriously, and promised someone would be at the hotel immediately.

That was why Paladin needed me. She was, as she once told me, a bulldozer, with no finesse at all. Sometimes I thought I was all finesse. But finesse was what we needed here to find the bomb (if there was one), catch the real culprit, and keep one of us from going to jail for instituting a bomb scare.

Not to mention the fen stampede if anyone mentioned the word "bomb" at a science fiction convention.

In the meantime, I contacted hotel security and convention security, neither of which were very secure.

Hotel security was two middle-aged guys so tough that I could probably take them one-handed, and con security was two old-timers and anyone who wanted to work for a free membership.

Which was how we ended up with Phil.

Who was really starting to panic.

***

Paladin was still crouching over the bomb, hand extended.

For the record, she hadn't discovered the bomb. She'd been checking the vulnerable areas—day care, kids programming, gaming—while both types of security scrounged the rest of the hotel, particularly the public areas, looking for "suspicious" items. In this, con security did better than hotel security. To hotel security, the whole damn convention looked suspicious.

But the bomb itself—well, that proved not so hard to find.

At least for me. Security—both kinds—had walked past it twice.

Seems we hadn't told them about the Pandora's Box label on the e-mail. It would have been helpful, since a small sign stood just behind the boxes reading…of all things…Pandora's Box.

I noticed it immediately, on my first pass through the hotel.

"I think if I move this," Paladin said, her hand a little closer to the box now.

"*No!*" we all said in unison.

"Seriously," she said. "It's not attached to anything. Besides, I think it's a secrets box—"

"*No!*" we said again.

"You guys are wussies," she said, then snatched the box, and sprinted for the stairs.

"Paladin!" I shouted. "Paladin!"

Stupid woman. Didn't she know that some bombs were motion sensitive? Some could be set off by cell phones? Some could—

I gave up arguing with her in my head and ran after her. No one else did, which was either just as dumb as my move or just as smart. The lower box could have blown when she picked up the upper box. The lower box could blow seconds from now. The upper box could blow at any moment—and she had to run through the lobby—and we would all die.

She took the stairs. I heard the door bang. Smart girl, not taking the elevator.

I hadn't run in—oh, maybe ever. I could hear my feet pounding and I was wheezing. I pulled open the door to the stairs and the only thing that kept me from pausing there to catch my breath was the thought of Paladin, dying because she did something stupid, something I could have prevented.

Like grabbing a bomb out of a hotel and running to the parking lot.

When I reached the top of the stairs, I heard another door bang, and then an emergency alarm go off.

She had gone out one of the side entrances instead of going through the lobby.

I clanged down the metal steps until I reached the door with the gigantic "Emergency Exit" sign emblazoned across its large metal handle. Above that sign were several more, warning that alarms would go off if the door was used unnecessarily.

Apparently they went off when it was used necessarily as well.

I pushed the door open and stepped into bright sunshine, which reminded me that I was hung-over and worse, I hadn't seen daylight from the outside for nearly three days.

Paladin had moved to an empty part of the parking lot—actually the parking lot of a nearby hotel—and had set the box down.

"Step away from it, Paladin," I shouted.

"Spade," she said. "I think I know how it works."

"Step away from it!" I shouted again, louder, even though I was getting closer to her.

"Spade, seriously—"

"Step away from the goddamn box," I shouted, swearing at her, which was something I had never ever done.

She didn't move. Instead, she looked at me in shock. "Stay back, Spade," she said. "If this thing goes, I don't want it to take you out."

I ran over to her, even though every bit of my flesh jiggled, even though my Evil Genius t-shirt was soaked, even though I was scared out of my mind.

I grabbed her arm and pulled her away, probably hurting her. I didn't care. She dug in, and I still didn't care. She was probably stronger than me, but I was *scared* and I had adrenalin on my side. Adrenalin and mass.

I won.

"Spade," she said. "Seriously—"

"No," I said. "I won't hear it. You're not going near that thing. You're lucky it wasn't motion sensitive. You're lucky—"

At that moment, my cell rang. Paladin looked at me as if she expected me to answer it. I expected me to answer it. It was probably the police.

But the minute I let go of her, she would run back to that damn device, thinking she really was a hero out of some old Western television show, and I would lose her forever.

"Get the cell out of my pocket, answer it, and put it to my ear," I said.

"I'm not your servant, Spade," she said.

"I don't care," I said. "Just do it."

She must have heard something in my voice she'd never heard before. Hell, *I* had heard something in my voice I'd never heard before. She grabbed the phone, pressed the screen and had to stand on her tiptoes to put the phone against my ear.

"Spade," I growled.

"Detective Harold Procalmeyer," said an unfamilar voice. "You mentioned an emergency and delicacy? I'm in the parking lot and—"

"Detective," I said with more relief than I expected. "Can you come to the north side of the building. I have something you need to see."

Paladin was watching me. Her entire body melted, just a little, as if she finally understood the risk she took. Or maybe she understood that I wasn't going to let her go, and the cop was going to thwart everything. Or maybe she just got hit with that lethargy people felt after the adrenalin rush ended.

The cop didn't say goodbye. He just hung up, and within minutes, he walked over—less Columbo and more modern American police detective, pressed khakis (who did that?), suit coat, military haircut—one of those manly men that I would have expected Paladin to prefer.

Instead, she stepped behind me like a scared kid, putting me between him and her.

"Detective?" I asked.

He nodded, showed me his badge, and I explained. I showed him the e-mail—now crumpled and soggy—then nodded toward the box in the middle of the empty parking lot.

I told him about the box upstairs, the fears I had, and I managed to sound like an authority.

He looked around my shoulder. "You're Paladin?" he asked her.

She nodded, leaning against me.

"You took a hell of a risk, young lady," he said, as if she were four. "You think I'm going to commend you, but I'm not. That bomb could have been motion sensitive. It could have been—"

130

"Spade gave me the lecture, thanks," she said. "And I still think we should do something about it."

"*We're* not going to do anything," he said. "I am."

And he did.

*****

CrapCon was the first con I'd ever worked where the bomb squad showed up—not that the attendees ever knew. The con went on as planned. The box upstairs, heavily guarded by hotel security and con security, turned out to be just a box, although it and the sign were taken away as evidence.

The smaller box—the artistic one? The one that Paladin ran with?—that really was a bomb.

Two guys dressed like the cast of the *Hurt Locker* inspected it, then covered it with some kind of blast-proof thingie, and used remote controls to detonate it.

Seems it was a secrets box, like Paladin thought. Only if you tried to get to the hidden compartment, ingredients flowed together like the ingredients were supposed to do on the failed London airplane bomb in 2007 or the failed Christmas Day bombing attempt here in the States in 2009. A little bit of this, a little bit of that, and kablooey! There would have been a hole where the second floor lobby was, lots of damage to the first floor lobby, and lots of injured or dead fen.

And, oh, yeah, Con Ops, where I usually lived, would have been destroyed.

Paladin and I retired there to wait for the police to finish their work. We watched a lot of it on the security monitors, while we noshed on everything room service could provide, from nachos to baby shrimp to buffalo wings. Apparently sheer terror made us both nervous.

"You have to tell me," I said after we replayed the explosion for the fifth time, "what this really was about."

She looked at me sideways. "How come you think I know anything about this?"

"Come on, Paladin," I said, too tired for finesse. "The e-mail came to you. The women on that lovely box all looked like you. This was about you, and I think you knew it before you even came to get me."

Her cheeks were red. "My hair isn't that long," she said. "And I would never wear clothes like that."

I waited.

"Don't you ever get weird e-mail?" she asked, almost plaintively.

Yes, I did. But it was all from friends. Clearly she'd been dealing with this longer than today.

"I trust you brought everything he sent you," I said.

"How do you know it's a he?" she asked.

I shrugged. "I don't know," I said. "But I don't think it's that big a guess."

***

Paladin had brought her entire laptop with everything in it, from the e-mails to invoices she had sent to clients five years ago. Paladin did not throw away anything.

While I set the laptop up next to the Tower of Terror, I talked. Mostly, I didn't want her to think I was invading her privacy, even though I was.

"Okay," I said. "Here's what we know. This guy is connected to fandom. He is either an artist or friends with an artist. He probably has a military background, although he could have some kind of chemistry or engineering background as well. He might be a scientist. And he thinks he knows Greek mythology."

"Thinks?" she said, hovering next to me. Even though we'd both been running and we hadn't had time to clean off, she still smelled faintly of soap. I smelled like a gamer at the end of a one-week tournament.

"Thinks," I said. "'Pandora's box' is wrong. Pandora—who was utterly beautiful, by the way, and whose name means 'all gifts'—arrived at Prometheus's doorstep with a jar, given to her by Zeus. The jar, which was probably as big as you, was initially used to store oil. Both Pandora and the jar were a gift to Prometheus, and the jar was to be Pandora's dowry. But Prometheus didn't trust Zeus for some strange reason, and gave Pandora along with her dowry to his brother, who took both woman and jar, and presumably opened both of them."

"Crude," Paladin said.

I shrugged. "Your friend did know what the mythological jar contained, however. He knew that the jar contained a cloud of evils that flew free the moment the jar got opened. Pandora clapped the lid back on the jar, trapping only hope inside. That's the reference."

Paladin sighed. "So maybe he knew the story after all, but just got the name wrong?"

I shook my head. "He only knew the vague details or he wouldn't have gone to all that trouble. He made a box because he thought that Pandora's box was right. And somehow he associates you with all the evils in the world."

"Oh, lucky me," she said.

"Any idea who it might be?" I asked.

She frowned. "It could be anyone," she said. "People don't really like me, Spade."

"Sure they do," I said, but I didn't really know that. I only knew that I liked her.

"I'm tough and blunt and bossy. I insult people and I run right through them if they get in my way. I don't have friends," she said.

"Except me," I said.

She looked over her shoulder at me, those luminescent eyes meeting mine, then assessing me for a very long time. I held my breath, not sure what she was doing—or what she was thinking.

"Except you," she said. Then she went back to staring at the laptop.

I stopped staring. I dug into its guts, tracking e-mails and looking for all kinds of information people didn't know they were sending when they sent things over the Internet.

While I dug into the laptop, I ran a search on the Tower of Terror, looking for artists, sculptors and dealers who handled art boxes. I cross-referenced that with military experience, as well as scientific experience or degrees, particularly those who then went on to work for the government in classified areas. Then I filtered it for men who lived, worked, or had worked on the West Coast. Paladin was known in the East and South, but mostly as a rumor. She did the bulk of her work west of the Mississippi.

I ran two other concurrent searches. I looked for fen who called themselves Prometheus or who liked to play with fire. And I looked for art boxes like the one the bomb had been made of for sale on sites like eBay.

It didn't take that long to find him.

"Dale Brewer, that son of a bitch," she said as she looked at the photo which appeared on my screen. The photo came from a con badge at one of the majors, done five years before.

Brewer wasn't at all what I expected—neat and trim and not bad looking in a Mirror Universe Spock kinda way. Dark hair, goatee, and that shiny-eyed precision that could either be the mark of brilliance or a serial killer or both.

"How do you know him?" I asked.

Her lips thinned. "He promised to help me find a room at my very first con," she said. "He said a bunch of people were sharing and all I needed was a sleeping bag. Turned out he picked a woman from that bunch and honored her by letting her sleep in the bedroom of a suite. With him. Alone."

"But you didn't do that," I said.

"I figured it out, told him no, and slept in my car. For years, he called me the one that got away. Then he got—I don't know—creepier, if that was possible, and the California cons banned him."

I checked my database. They didn't ban him. They flagged him because several women had gotten restraining orders against him. Apparently he wasn't allowed within 200 yards of any con those women attended. None of the women were Paladin, at least that I could tell, not without knowing her real name.

I didn't tell her that. I just nodded.

She pushed away from the Tower of Terror and reached for her laptop.

I caught her hand. It was tiny and warm in my huge sweaty one. "What're you doing?" I asked.

"I'm going to let Mr. Dale Brewer know what I think of his little prank," she said.

"First, Paladin, it wasn't a prank. Second, he has explosives training from the U.S. Army, and then he went to work for the DoD until they asked him to leave. He made his living designing these boxes—out of resin—which can be used to transport bombs. The name on his badge at the last two conventions he was allowed to attend was The SF Unabomber. You don't want to get near his house."

She glared at me, then crossed those magnificent arms. "Oh, but I do."

"He knows you pretty well, right?" I asked.

She nodded. "He's kept his eye on me."

"So he knows you're a bulldozer."

Her frown got deeper. It wasn't so much a frown now as a suspicious look. "So?"

"So, he's going to expect you to come after him. Physically. He's planned for it. He's *prepared.*"

When she ran with that bomb, I let her see how scared I was. I let her see it afterwards too. But I didn't let her see it now, because she'd gone all Tough Chick on me. I was afraid my fear would push her into action.

"I can put him in prison for a long time," I said. "I can make sure he doesn't bother anyone again. And I can do it without involving you or fandom or CrapCon."

"How?" she asked.

I patted the Tower of Terror. "I work with the police all over the country—"

"On forensic accounting cases," she said. She knew because she'd helped me with one.

"I have bona fides," I said. "My evidence is good stuff. And what I have here is evidence, Paladin. The kind juries *love.*"

"Why won't I have to be involved?" she asked. "He sent the e-mail to me. I took the bomb outside. The box looks like me, for heaven's sake."

She wouldn't normally have admitted that and probably already regretted the words.

"We don't need motive," I said. "There's more than enough physical evidence. The cops are going to eat this up. Trust me on this, Paladin."

***

She did.

The cops arrested Brewer half an hour after getting my information, which I hand-delivered as a way to escape CrapCon which was steadily going downhill.

When I got back, the hospitality suite was being picketed because it had run out of Blue Goo, and no one was smart enough to go to the local liquor store to get more. I dispatched the head of the con—which was a stupid name for such an incompetent person—and let her make the Blue Goo when she got back.

I ignored the panels, such as they were, prevented the masquerade from turning into a food fight, and started the Renaissance Dance early. Then I took a much-needed shower and returned to Con Ops, to find a huge cup of coffee, a coupon for Krispy Kremes and a note from Paladin.

> *This isn't nearly payment enough for all the help. But I got a call that couldn't wait, so I'll catch you next time. I owe you, Spade.*
>
> *XXOO*
> *Paladin*

Of course I saved the note. And not in my pocket where it could get all sweaty and the ink would run. But in my wallet, where I could pull it out and stare at those "xx"s and "oo"s, and try to figure out if she meant them.

I spent weeks thinking about them in fact, long after CrapCon got relegated to fannish history, long after the local SMoFs told the local fans that they would never support another CrapCon again—and this was without me telling anyone about the bomb scare.

I actually thought about those "xx"s and "oo"s for months. In fact, I was still thinking about them when I had to testify at Dale Brewer's trial.

The idiot didn't take a plea. He seemed to think he could charm a jury. He couldn't, of course. They convicted in less than an hour, and never even learned that he had targeted a science fiction convention. Just that his bomb was placed in a hotel during a convention, and fortunately, the device hadn't triggered. He got convicted on attempted murder, domestic terrorism, and a host of smaller charges.

I was in court for the verdict. I wanted to see the son of a bitch, as Paladin called him, get his comeuppance. In person he reminded me even more of the Mirror Universe Spock—tall, thin, with eyes that pierced.

In that short time between the call back and the jury filing in, Dale Brewer turned in his seat, his arm resting on the railing separating the gallery from the defense table. His lawyer tried to catch his attention, but she couldn't.

He was looking for me.

His smile was cold.

"The Great Spade," he said. "You can't always protect her."

"She doesn't need protecting," I said, knowing I shouldn't engage.

"Really?" he said.

"Really," I said. "She's the most capable person I know."

He nodded once, then turned back. And as the jury filed in, he seemed to forget about me.

I wished I could forget about him, with his back-to-back life sentences. But I couldn't entirely.

Because that smile was so cold.

And because he called himself the SF Unabomber.

And because he made boxes—boxes that mixed explosives when you touched the right part.

I warned Paladin, of course. And she listened because she trusts me.

But I go into sf conventions now and troll the dealer's room for boxes, arty boxes, the kind that you could hide a ring in or a note. Or an explosive.

So far I haven't found anything. But I know I will one day.

And I'm going to make sure that no one buys it.

Paladin says that Brewer did open a Pandora's box—in my head.

She's right, of course. He sent out a little cloud of evil, the kind that will keep me looking at boxes from now until the last convention I ever attend.

But Paladin doesn't know one thing. A cloud of evil wasn't all that came out of that box. There was hope too.

Which I keep in my wallet, except in those moments of weakness when I need to look at the "xx"s and "oo"s.

TRICK OR TREAT

SOMETIMES IN THE mundane world, I feel like a fish out of water. But on that Halloween day, driving my Lexus SUV in a part of San Francisco I had never seen before, I felt like a whale covered in bling with a target on his back—and, oh yeah, in need of water Real Soon Now.

It was my own fault. Over the years, I'd driven all over San Francisco in search of convention hotels—approving, disapproving, looking for bargains, seeing why the hotels really were bargains—and I knew better than to drive a high-end rental in certain parts of the city.

The problem is that I usually need high-end rentals for their size. I'm 6'6" and four hundred pounds on a good day. After the month I'd had, I was probably four hundred and forty pounds because I'd had to buy new jeans and haul out the XXXXL t-shirts that I'd packed away for emergencies.

And now things could get worse. The last thing I wanted was some gang to car-jack me at an intersection.

I had no doubt that they'd toss me out of the SUV (shoe-horn me out of the SUV?), but I suspected they just might shoot me when they saw the shirt. It had been a giveaway from the twenty-year anniversary promotion of the movie *Alien*, and it had a little rubber alien head bursting out of the chest.

I was wearing the shirt with two conflicting expectations. First, I hoped that the folks at the shelter would think it was a great (if subtle) Halloween costume; and second, I figured Paladin would force me to wear the shelter's service t-shirt whether I arrived in a tux or arrived in my underwear. I had volunteered at shelters on special occasions in the past, and they almost always had special clothing requirements (usually that I had to purchase).

If I had given this little detour more thought, I would have dressed a lot more sedately and I would have borrowed some book dealer's ratty van. Paladin was asking me to help out at a shelter, for godssake, which meant that by definition I was heading to a relatively crappy neighborhood.

But I was preoccupied with my role as Savior of Alternate Pro-Con, which wasn't really the name of the convention or my real title. If you're involved in science fiction fandom, you know which upstart pro-con I'm talking about, but for the rest of you, here's a bit of a clue.

There are only a handful of pro-cons every year in the science fiction community, and only two over Halloween weekend. "Pro-con" is shorthand for "professional convention," and it is designed for just the professionals in the field, from the writers to the editors. I suppose actors and producers and gaming company employees could come too, but they almost never do, because what's the point of them showing up to promote things without a fan presence?

As you can probably tell from my tone, the very name "pro-con" irritates me. For me, all sf conventions are professional venues, since I work when I'm at them. I am what is known of as a Secret Master of Fandom, one of the small group of fans who run science fiction conventions. That may sound minor to those of you who have never been to an sf convention, but think of it this way: a convention forms for one weekend and, in that weekend, generates millions of dollars in revenue.

The bigger conventions generate the most revenue. That's the other thing about pro-cons, they really don't earn much more than the initial fees. Writers don't splurge in the dealers' room, and publishers don't see a need to have a booth. The restaurants and bars do bang-up business, but on a revenue side, a pro-con is generally a bust.

I know this because I generally handle the finances for dozens of conventions per year. Among my many titles is forensic accountant, but that's not why most cons bring me in.

They bring me in because I'm what's known of in Pacific Northwest parlance as a rarity: I'm a Microsoft Millionaire who managed to grow the fortune he got when he "retired" from the early days of Microsoft. Most Microsoft Millionaires—who got their millions before

Microsoft figured out that paying in stock wasn't a good idea—are now Microsoft Poorionaires (also a Pacific NW term) because they divested the stock and spent the money about twenty years ago.

Because I still have funds, because I love numbers, and because I really, really love sf conventions, I became the go-to financial guy in the sf world. Ultimately, that made me a SMoF. In the end, though, it's my ability to quietly solve crimes that occur in and around conventions that has made me famous and has given me the moniker almost everyone knows me by: Spade.

As I mentioned, I don't like pro-cons, and the fact I was working one of the worst annoyed the hell out of me. No one dressed up at a pro-con—at least, not in an sf costume. (They wore business suits.) There wasn't a dance or a masquerade. No one discussed TV or movies or games, unless they talked about selling to those venues. There was nothing fannish at a pro-con, and fannish was what I liked about conventions.

Once upon a time, there was only one pro-con on Halloween weekend. But a few years back, some disgruntled pros who couldn't get into the long-running World Fantasy Convention (which limits its attendance) decided that they needed to have their own pro-con on the same weekend.

These pros cornered some like-minded fans, and that was how Alternate Pro-Con as I'm calling it came about.

Like WFC, Alternate Pro-Con has a "literary" bent, albeit not restricted just to the fantasy genre. Alternate

Pro-Con decided to be ecumenical and include science fiction, not that that boosted attendance much. It just added a few more options for its juried award which it also patterned on the World Fantasy Award.

I don't think I told Paladin about my hatred of pro-cons and of Alternate Pro-Con in particular, but I'm also not the kind of guy who can hide his emotions easily. And when I arrived in San Francisco, Paladin's home base, I suspect she got the message about my dislike of the entire process pretty damn quick.

I contacted Paladin just before I arrived. I don't have any special access to her, no secret cell phone number, no address hastily scrawled on the back of her business card. Instead, I have to do what everyone else does: write an e-mail to Paladin@paladinsanfrancisco.com.

I don't even know her real name. I call her Paladin, just like everyone else does. The only specialized knowledge I have about her comes from my own geekiness: I'm familiar with the fifty-year-old Richard Boone television series *Have Gun, Will Travel* from which she took her name. I know that because her business card (which I keep in my wallet for emergencies) uses the quotes from the Boone character's card:

Have Gun, Will Travel
Wire Paladin
San Francisco

Only her card says "e-mail" instead of "wire."

It took me longer than expected to get to the shelter, even though I rolled through every single stop sign in the neighborhood. It was a lot farther away from the con than I expected. And then the shelter itself surprised me.

I had expected an old Victorian house, like so many houses in San Francisco. Something like an expanded Queen Anne, with an extra turret or a palatial (if rundown) former mansion cocked sideways on a hillside.

The shelter was cocked sideways on a hillside (what wasn't in San Francisco?), but it wasn't a remodeled house at all. It was a still-active church.

I never pegged Paladin as a church-going type.

The church did have a parking lot right next door, and the parking lot had a wire fence around it, but no guard and no hidden parking place. I declined to drive in, going to the pick-up-and-receiving area in back.

Like I expected, the church's kitchen door was open, and a junkie sat on the stoop, smoking a cigarette.

"Ain't nobody can park here," he said as I pulled up.

My face flushed. I felt like the rich guy that I was, and I was acting like some entitled rich guy, like the stupid pros I complained about at the Alternate Pro-Con. But I wasn't going to let anyone strip my Lexus rental for parts, not on this afternoon anyway.

"I'm helping with deliveries," I said as I got out of the SUV, and wondered if that were true. Paladin hadn't really told me what I'd be doing. She said the shelter was handling a special event for Halloween and she needed my help with it.

Special events could be anything from something modeled on Trick-Or-Treat For UNICEF or a special Halloween meal for folks who shouldn't be on the street or a special party for the kids lucky enough to have shelter that night. I had no idea and I had been too self-involved to ask.

The junkie tossed his still-glowing cigarette into a nearby puddle. Then he stood, wiped his hands on his jeans, and extended one hand to me.

"Reverend Harvey," he said.

My flush deepened. My bad, thinking this guy was a junkie just because he was beyond thin and smoking on the stoop.

"My friends call me Spade," I said.

"Ah," Reverend Harvey said. "Paladin told me to expect you. You want a safe place to park your car."

I didn't think the flush could get any more painful, but it did. "It's not my car," I said, as if that mattered. "It's a rental."

"Yeah," Reverend Harvey said. "We're not in the best of neighborhoods, but no one bothers with vehicles connected with the church. You can leave it here for now."

"Thanks," I muttered. Sometimes I felt really stupid, particularly when dealing with regular people. It didn't matter that I had such a high I.Q. that I was in the point-one percentile. Brain smarts didn't always equal people smarts. I had people-smarts for someone active in fandom, but the folks in the mundane world—that's the non-fannish world for those of you in the non-fannish world—had greater people skills than I could ever hope to achieve.

Then I realized that Reverend Harvey's grammar had improved tremendously. "Ain't nobody can park here" was quite a different sentence from "You want a safe place to park your car." Different in grammar, different in tone, different in education level.

My flush faded, and it took all of my strength not to give the man a piercing look.

I knew some people who worked the streets used a different language for each audience, but Reverend Harvey had used two different languages with me. It made me uncomfortable, as if he was playing at something.

Maybe he was. Maybe the first time, he was trying to get rid of the obnoxious fat white guy, and maybe the second time, he realized that the obnoxious fat white guy had money to tap for the shelter.

I let out a small breath and reminded myself not to be too cynical. After all, Paladin worked with these people. She knew who they were better than anyone else, and she was the one who told me to come down here.

I followed Reverend Harvey into a huge church kitchen. The place smelled of garlic and frying hamburger. I saw at least three stoves, and two large refrigerators as well as a door leading into a freezer, and another into a pantry. Those doors had open padlocks hanging from their handles.

Of course, a church that doubled as a shelter had to protect its most precious commodity: its food. Standing at a long table, a number of people chopped lettuce, onions, tomatoes, and other raw vegetables. Those volunteers wore jeans and a black t-shirt with a cross on the chest and the name of the church emblazoned across the back. I hoped I didn't have to wear one of those to serve a meal here. I wasn't affiliated with any religion outside of fandom itself, and I wanted it to stay that way.

I didn't see Paladin among them. Reverend Harvey said hello to a number of people, but didn't introduce me. He walked through the kitchen and out the double doors. I followed.

We entered some kind of gigantic room. I'd call it a recreation space, or a place for church suppers, but that might have been its original function. Now it held cots folded up against the wall, piles of clothing and bedding in the corner, and several volunteers setting up tables and metal folding chairs. A group of people in Halloween costumes gathered near one of the doors, and as I approached, one of them caught my eye.

It was a slight woman with the posture of a dancer. She wore a glittery fairy tale gown and held a sparkling blue wand. Her long black hair trailed down her back.

Then she turned around, and I gasped.

It was Paladin, dressed like a girl. She even wore glitter makeup. The look accented her elfin features, and the hair was tucked behind her naturally pointed ears. That long black hair had to be a wig. I'd seen her just a few months before, and her blonde hair then had been cropped short.

But the long hair suited her. So did the makeup and the outfit.

She was breathtakingly beautiful.

"What, Spade, you never seen a costume before?" she asked. The question—and the attitude—was all Paladin.

"I expected to see you in a brocade vest and cowboy boots, carrying a Peacemaker," I said.

"That was last year." She waved her wand and said to the group around her. "Meet me at the stairs in five."

They nodded. Finally, I spared them a glance, and realized they were mostly kids. They carried buckets with the name of the shelter on it, and another, smaller bucket marked "candy."

"I thought you might be doing something like Trick or Treat for UNICEF," I said.

"Actually," Reverend Harvey said, "they're going to work a major convention downtown. Lots of city fathers will be there, and we should be able to coax a few donations out of them."

"What am I supposed to do? Drive?" I asked.

Paladin looked at Reverend Harvey. "Give us a minute, Reverend, okay?"

"Surely," Reverend Harvey said, half bowing to her. Then he headed back into the kitchen. I uncharitably wondered if he was going back for another cigarette.

"I got another job for you." Paladin put her small warm hand on my bare arm.

A jolt of electricity went through me, and that damn flush returned. I tried to pretend that her hand didn't have an effect on me.

"Come with me." She led me through a different set of doors and across a hallway. Then she pushed open a door marked "Ladies," but didn't go inside.

"Vamoose," she said through the open door, and clapped her hands.

I said, "Paladin—"

"Shush," she said to me as half a dozen girls in various states of undress walked out. The girls seemed resigned, as if they got tossed out of the ladies room all the time. "Come on."

Paladin stepped inside. I had no choice. I followed.

The inside wasn't a bathroom. It was a dressing room—kinda. It had several full-length mirrors, many chairs, a couch, and some glazed windows with gold crosses across them. Piles of clothes, backpacks and purses sat haphazardly against the chairs and wall.

Once I was inside, Paladin opened another door. Through that, I saw stalls. "Everyone out?" she asked.

Her voice echoed and no one answered. So she went back to the main door, and turned a deadbolt I hadn't even noticed.

"I need you to babysit," she said.

"In here?" I asked, feeling panicked.

"No," she said with irritation, as if I had put her off her game. She looked toward the only door that she hadn't opened.

"I don't do kids," I said.

"I know that," she said with even greater irritation. "Do you think I would ask if you were that kind of man."

I bristled for a moment—how dare she even think of me in that way? We'd worked a pedophile case together—and then I instantly calmed down. Of course, she would make that assumption from the sentence I spoke. She worked with runaways and abuse victims all the time. Her sf convention work was the anomaly, not the norm.

"I meant," I said with an infinite patience I didn't feel, "I don't deal with kids in any way."

"Too bad," she said. "I need you to take a kid to the convention for the day."

"Paladin, it's not that kind of convention. There isn't even kid's programming or more than the hotel-provided childcare area. I can't—"

"I know what Alternate Pro-Con is, Spade," she said with so much irritation that I was amazed she wasn't spitting as she talked. "She can hang with you in Ops."

Ops was convention operations, where I made my base. Usually I spent more time in Ops during a convention than I ever spent in my hotel room.

"Paladin," I said, matching her irritation. "Kids don't belong in Ops—wait. Did you say *she*?"

"I did," Paladin said, "and she's not really a kid. She's thirteen. She—"

"That's worse, Paladin," I said. "One reason I don't get in trouble is that I don't put myself in awkward situations that could cause even the slightest misunderstanding, and having a lifelong somewhat weird bachelor take care of a thirteen-year-old girl he's not related to is one of those awkward situations that could be misconstrued."

"Trust me, this won't get misconstrued," she said, glancing at that door again.

"The worst situations in the world always start with the words, 'trust me,'" I said. "I'm sorry, Paladin, but you'll need to find—"

"*I need your help,*" she said with an intensity I've never heard from her. Rather than yelling, she had lowered her voice, but the words still felt like daggers. "You always told me that I could trust you, that you're my friend. I don't have friends, Spade, except for you, but I have an understanding of them that mostly comes from literature and buddy movies, and those things always say that when your friend asks you to jump, you say, 'How high?'"

I frowned. "That's not quite what friendship is, Paladin. It's less about giving orders than it is about volunteering."

"Well, then, never mind. See what I care." She waved a hand. "Get out then. I'll figure out something else."

She seemed on edge and desperate. I'd never seen Paladin desperate before.

"How long do I have to babysit?" I asked.

"What?" she said, as if I had already left, and I was contacting her from the great beyond. "Oh, um, until later tonight. Two meals, Spade, and maybe a video on your iPad or something. Ten hours max."

"And you'll come get her?" I asked.

"I'll come get her," Paladin said.

"And you'll vouch for me if something goes wrong?" I asked.

She looked at me, a single crease in her glittery forehead. "What could possibly go wrong?"

I hated that question more than almost any other. That question, combined with "trust me" led to bad decisions. And there I was, making one of them.

Because I agreed to babysit, as Paladin called it.

"Okay," I said. "Tell me why we're hiding in here and why you're so tense."

"I don't have time for that," she said. "I gotta get those other kids to that stupid gala."

"Paladin," I said, ready to back out all over again.

"Here's what happens, Spade. She's in that back room. I have a sheet over her head with some eyes cut out of it. You and me and her are going to join my trick-or-treat group, and I'll lead us outside. I'll take the group to my van, and a few others will go in your car. You'll drop off everyone but your little ghost at the gala."

"Do I get to know her name?" I asked, my stomach clenching.

"Sure," Paladin said. "Call her Casper."

"Seriously, Paladin—"

"She's going to call you Spade. That's not your real name. She calls me Paladin. That's not my real name. So you get to call her Casper, which is the name she chose. Believe me, it's better than Wednesday, which is the name I had to talk her out of."

"Because you don't like the Addams Family?" I asked.

"Because I thought naming yourself after a day of the week was too confusing," Paladin said. "Jeez, Spade, can you make this any more difficult?"

"No, Paladin," I snapped. "Can you?"

We glared at each other for a minute. Her glittery cheeks were flushed. I found myself wondering if this was our first fight, and if it was, did that mean our friendship had progressed to a new place or did it mean that our friendship was in jeopardy?

Then I sighed.

"Okay," I said, backing down. Of course, we both knew that I would be the one to back down. I had more invested in this relationship—at least, I thought I did. "We'll follow Plan A. Is there a Plan B?"

"I'm working on that," she said.

***

Plan A went off without a hitch. Me and my Friendly Ghost joined Paladin's trick-or-treat group and headed out the front of the church. I knew little about Casper except that she was quiet and tiny and smelled of Bazooka Bubblegum, a smell I hadn't encountered for years.

She and four other ghosts, who seemed to be thin and male, joined me in the Lexus, and we followed Paladin's white panel van to some large fancy restaurant near Fisherman's Wharf. Once we arrived, Paladin gathered all of the ghosts except Casper. Then she handed me one of her business cards with a cell phone number written on the back.

"In case of emergency," she said, and then she herded her little troupe into the restaurant.

Emergency. I didn't like that word.

"You ever been to a science fiction convention?" I asked Casper as we drove away.

She shrugged her shoulders—or at least, I thought she shrugged. The sheet moved up and down. Then the head turned, and the eyes focused out the passenger window.

I had been dismissed.

I didn't mind. I needed time to think. Something was up, something important. Paladin wanted this kid hidden for a few hours, so I would hide her, whatever it took.

I decided it wouldn't be as hard as babysitting 500 science fiction professionals.

And on that, at least, I was right.

***

I got back to Con Ops to find Betty Jo Smeerly arguing with Doris Xavier. Doris ran security at almost every convention where I was Lord of Finance. I'd brought her in here because she was local, and because I needed a familiar face on the convention team.

Casper trailed behind me like a…well, you figure it out. She stopped at the door of Con Ops as if she had never seen anything like it before—and she probably hadn't.

By this point in a convention, Ops usually smelled like BO, three-day old pizza, and sour ice cream. This Ops didn't, though, because this convention wasn't a traditional science fiction convention. The pros caused trouble, but not the same kind as fans. And the pros either went to programming or they went out to eat with their editors. Things got rough after midnight when the hotel bar closed, and the pros who couldn't stop drinking sat in the con suite and sucked up the free beer.

We usually had fights then, but they were over things like careers and book covers and who slept with whose spouse. You know, the stuff that professional business people of all stripes fought about.

I preferred fan conventions which could come to blows over important things like which Klingon greeting was appropriate for a Classic Star Trek party as opposed to a Next Generation party.

"What the heck's going on?" I said as I stepped inside.

Everyone jumped except Casper, who seemed immune. Or maybe she kept her jumpiness inside.

One of the volunteer staff—someone I didn't know, who had probably been recruited by the local sf people at the last minute—went around me, and closed the door.

So the fight was important and politically dicey.

"Betty Jo won't administer the awards," Doris said tightly.

I hadn't known it was Betty Jo's job to administer the awards, but I generally stayed away from anything to do with awards. Awards made professional writers crazy. They also made the award staff crazy, but not for the same reasons.

"I'm sorry I asked," I said as I headed toward my Tower of Terror.

The Tower of Terror was my computer system. State-of-the-art, networked to everything except the Department of Defense (and sometimes I wasn't even sure about that), my computer system had everything, from its own routers and servers and Internet connection to more backup than you'd find at Microsoft on any given day.

I ran dozens of conventions out of this thing, and used it for all kinds of forensic analysis. It wasn't my only computer system. I had five laptops and four tablets with me, as well as seven duplicate Towers of Terror and other gadgets at home. I updated all my devices every six months whether I needed to or not, and I tried to stay ahead of the latest, latest, latest everything.

But the Tower of Terror wasn't my main objective at the moment. My main objective was my chair. I had four chairs specially made for my frame, and one got shipped to any convention I worked. Doris called my chair the Captain's Chair after Kirk's chair in the original *Star Trek*, partly because my chair had so many buttons and knobs and special gadgets of its own that, on a good day, it could probably work the Tower of Terror without me.

I wanted my chair like a little kid wanted his blankie. I was tired and tense, and I had a silent little ghost trailing me everywhere.

"You aren't going to settle this fight?" the con guy I didn't know whispered.

"It's an awards' fight," I said. "I'll lose."

"There's a tie," Betty Jo said loudly, so that I could hear. "In fact, there's two ties."

I nodded tiredly. I turned to Casper, who was standing beside me. "You look hot," I said. "You want a soda or something?"

I figured getting her a soda was easier than asking her to take off the sheet.

The sheet went up and down again. The kid's silence was bothering me.

"Well, I do," I said. "You wanna get me a Diet Coke, and pick up something for yourself? There's a bunch of sodas in that cooler over there."

She didn't say anything, just glided toward the cooler as if she could float.

"I mean," Betty Jo said, "we can't give out the award until we know who actually won."

"Ties happen," I said, then bit my lip. I did not want to get involved, but I couldn't seem to shut up.

"That's what I've been telling her," Doris said.

"Ties do not happen when there's a five-person jury!" Betty Jo said.

I glanced at the kid. She was peering at the cooler, but I couldn't tell if she hovered over it because she couldn't see very good or because she couldn't figure out whether she should just grab something from it or because she didn't see anything she liked.

I sighed. "Someone probably recused themselves."

I was lying. Doris and I both knew it, but maybe that would stop the stupid fight.

"No one did," Betty Jo said. "I polled the jury."

Great. A conscientious administrator. That wasn't helpful.

"No, you did not," I said, with emphasis, hoping she understood me.

"But I did," she said.

Great. A conscientious *clueless* administrator.

"Ties happen *all the time* at Alternate Pro-Con," I said. "Ties happen with juried awards."

"Not on my watch," Betty Jo said.

"Yes, on your watch," I said. "Because if this tie doesn't go through—"

"These *ties*," she said.

"—then you'll never be allowed at Alternate Pro-Con again."

She stared at me, eyes narrowed. I had succeeded in diverting her attention at least. She was mad—at me. "You won't let me in?"

"I'm not the administrator," I said. "I'm just a SMoF flunky who got drafted to keep this thing together."

Her frown deepened. "Then how do you know I won't be able to come here again if I fix the tie?"

"Jeez," a little voice said, a voice I didn't recognize. "Lady, pay attention. He's telling you the vote is rigged."

We all looked in the direction of the soda cooler.

Casper had spoken.

***

I didn't think I'd ever heard Con Ops so quiet this early in a convention. We were all staring at the little ghost clutching my Diet Coke. The sheet had come up far enough to reveal two scrawny legs housed in jeans so faded that they looked like they wouldn't survive another washing. Knobby ankles rose above ancient tennis shoes with holes along one side.

Casper peered at us through the holes cut in the sheet, then sighed loudly, and tossed the sheet backwards, narrowly missing the food and coffee table. She wore a t-shirt with a picture of Einstein on it, and I would have thought she was a boy if I hadn't already known she was a girl. Or I would have if it weren't for one other thing, something that made my breath catch.

With her obviously self-cut hair, her pixyish features, and her slightly pointed ears, she looked just like Paladin must have at the same age. Paladin in miniature: Just as tough, just as smart, and just as prickly.

"Who're you?" Betty Jo finally managed. She had her hands on her hips and was facing Casper.

"Casper." Then Casper bent down and started rummaging through the cooler, clearly looking for something she liked.

Betty Jo looked nonplussed. She kept staring at Casper for a minute, clearly not used to being ignored. Casper was doing a good job at avoiding her though, so finally Betty Jo turned to me.

"Who is she?" Betty Jo asked.

"She told you," I said, wishing Betty Jo would go away.

"Yes, but why is she here?" Betty Jo asked.

"She's with me," I said.

"Why?" Betty Jo asked. "This isn't a fan con."

I couldn't say that she was my niece, because that was too creepy-weird-uncle-with-roving-hands; I couldn't say she was my protégé, because that wasn't much better; I couldn't say I was watching her for a friend, because the mood Betty Jo was in that might cause more trouble.

So I said the first thing that came to mind. "I needed her help on something."

And that, at an sf convention, was an acceptable answer. We fen had all known long ago that kids held the keys to many kingdoms, often kingdoms we wanted to stay in for the rest of our already-misspent lives.

Casper looked at me sideways, still bent at the waist over the cooler. I had clearly surprised her. Which meant she hadn't spent a lot of time in fandom.

But Betty Jo wasn't surprised. She grunted and moved on, not happy about the awards, and no longer caring about Casper.

"Someone want to open that door?" I said. "It's getting hot in here."

Then I booted up the Tower of Terror, and pretended to get to work.

The door opened, and cooler air blew in. There was a sigh and a bang, followed by voices in the hallway. Betty Jo had left.

Doris moved into my range of vision. *Thanks*, she mouthed. I nodded.

And then it was quiet. Casper brought me my Diet Coke. She had popped it open away from the computers (great kid, that), and then set it in the cup holder on the arm of my chair without being asked.

In her other hand, she carried a cream soda. I didn't know that anyone made cream sodas any more. She stood just behind me, out of my line of sight. But she was reflected in my screen.

I worked on the project I'd been avoiding—organizing the convention's exceedingly messy books. I'd scanned and uploaded paper files. Now I was using a program of my own design to pull information from those digitized scraps of paper into an accounting spreadsheet.

I figured I'd do this for about ten minutes, and then I'd ask Casper if she wanted something to eat.

About five minutes in, she said, "You were lying about needing my help."

I leaned back and folded my hands over my ample belly, the way I imagined Nero Wolfe would have done in the same situation.

"It depends," I said. "I'm not sure what your skill levels are. You're certainly not top-notch wait staff."

She frowned, and straightened her shoulders. I still hadn't turned around. That seemed to bother her as well.

"I brought your Diet Coke," she said defensively.

"You did," I said. "Eight minutes after I asked for it."

"I didn't know there was a time limit."

"I didn't know it took eight minutes to get something out of that cooler." I waited. Smart and geeky with attitude usually didn't like being pandered to. So I was trying a different tack. I was being deliberately difficult.

She didn't say anything, but she didn't move either. I swiveled my chair slightly. Her cheeks were red—something that hadn't shown up on my screen—and I realized then that she was frozen in place. The attitude covered a superbrain nearly paralyzed with fear.

She was afraid to make mistakes, thought it dangerous. Dammit.

"How about something to eat?" I asked.

Casper shrugged. "It's okay. You don't have to feed me."

"Well, I will have to feed me," I said, "and it seems logical to feed you at that time as well."

"When you're ready," she said. Then she took a step closer to my computer. "Where did you get that program?"

I looked at the screen. Information was flying off the scanned paper and onto the spreadsheet—literally. I had devised the thing to look like the bits of information were little flying things (a variety of birds, paper airplanes, flying toasters, and whatever else I could think of) just to amuse myself. But I was so far past amusement on this convention project that I had forgotten that I had done that.

"I designed it," I said.

Her eyes lit up. "You did?"

I had actually impressed her. That felt like as much of a gift as Paladin's trust. "Yeah."

Casper took a step closer. "Can I borrow it?"

"The program?"

She nodded.

"You don't have a computer," I said.

Her shoulders went down. Expressive things, those shoulders. "Oh, yeah."

"But you can borrow one of mine." I grabbed a laptop from the shelf under the desk.

As I swung around with the laptop in my hands, Casper's eyes followed the laptop like it was food and she hadn't eaten in three days.

"Wow," she said. "I didn't even think that was in stores yet."

"It's not," I said. "I get a lot of prototypes. I used to work for Microsoft."

That explanation was usually enough for people, but Casper didn't let it go. "I know old guys who used to work for Microsoft. They don't get free computers."

I shrugged. "You want it or not?"

"Yeah," she said. "And the program too."

"It's already loaded onto the laptop." Although no other proprietary information was. I hadn't used that laptop yet for anything except prep.

"OMG," she said, enunciating each letter separately. I'd seen OMG in texts for years (it meant Oh My God), and I knew that some kids had taken texting slang into their verbal vocabulary, but this was the first time I'd ever heard anyone say it. "This is like sooo amazing."

Then she cradled the laptop in her arms as if it was a baby, and sank to the floor, crossing her legs as she went down. Oh, to be that young and in shape. Then she whipped a flash drive out of her pocket and stuck it into the laptop. I almost complained. I didn't want her to download the program for her own use. But I figured I'd check the flash drive before she left rather than alienate her now.

She hunched over the laptop as if nothing else existed.

I turned my chair a little so that I could see her without resorting to screen tricks. Then I monitored my own personal financial hell, while Casper typed and muttered and frowned at the screen in front of her.

I had no idea what she was doing, and I didn't want to know. Besides, if I wanted to, I could recreate everything she did when I got the laptop back.

I doubted I would want to. After all, what could a thirteen-year-old do that was interesting to me?

Or so I thought at the time.

***

About four hours in, I ordered pizza. I was going to order through room service. I even handed the room service menu to Casper. She took it distractedly, finished whatever she was typing, then gave the menu the same level of concentration she had been giving the laptop.

After a few minutes, she asked, "Did they screw up? Sweetbreads are in the entrées."

That was when I looked at the menu. Not only was it expensive (which I really didn't care about), it was highbrow, with nothing that really looked good. I didn't want to eat off that menu, and I doubted she did either.

So I told her what sweetbreads were, and she made a face that I doubted anyone else could have replicated. Then she said, "God, Hannibal Lecter would have loved eating here," which gave her a special place in my heart.

"You mind if I order pizza?" I asked.

"I do if it's from that menu," she said. "They'll probably put brains on it or something."

I grinned. "They probably would. But I know of a good place near here that delivers."

We did the normal negotiating that everyone did when figuring out what to put on a pizza. We were the only two people in the room, although we did order one extra pizza in case that guy whose name I didn't know returned or in case Doris decided to join us.

"Let's move the laptop off the floor," I said. "I'll move one of the chairs over to the desk."

"I like the floor," Casper said.

"Yeah, but someone might walk on the laptop," I said.

She picked it up, closed the lid and cradled it as if it was the most precious thing she had ever held. Then she frowned at me.

"Mind if I ask you a question?"

"Go ahead," I said.

Her frown deepened, and she said, "Do you get mad if numbers don't add up?"

"Numbers always add up for me," I said distractedly. Her question made me look at my screen. "I have had a gift for math for as long as I remember."

"No," she said. "I mean, do you get mad if someone else's numbers don't add up?"

That was when I realized the question was important. I swiveled my chair away from my screen and gave her my full attention.

"Sometimes," I said. "When I'm supposed to figure out why the numbers aren't working right, and someone hasn't given me the right information."

"Do you get mad at the person who told you the numbers don't add up?" She was holding the laptop so tightly that I half expected it to squeal.

"Usually no one has to tell me," I said. "Usually I'm telling someone else."

"Do they get mad at you then?" she asked.

"Yeah, sometimes," I said, resisting the urge to ask why she wanted to know this. If Casper was like Paladin, she wasn't going to give up information easily.

"Do they hit you?"

My mouth dropped open, and I almost asked her who had hit her, but I knew better. Suddenly an old conversation with Paladin flashed through my mind. We'd been sitting in a restaurant the first time I met her, and she told me: *I need your logical brain. You understand subtleties. I do not. I'm more of a bulldozer. I barge in, get the job done, and stomp out. That's not your reputation at all. You see things that no one else sees.*

Every interaction we'd had since then had reinforced Paladin's assessment of herself. She *was* a bulldozer. And the question I almost asked Casper was a bulldozer question.

Suddenly I wondered if my function here was more than that of a babysitter.

"No," I said. "People don't hit me. But I'm fairly big."

"Yeah," Casper said. "But you don't look muscle-y. You're squishy."

Squishy. I wasn't as offended as I should have been. Squishy was a better word than flabby.

"I'm still pretty big," I said gently. "People usually don't mess with me."

"Even when you tell them they're stupid," she said.

"Even then," I said, repressing a smile. "Although the mistakes I find are usually not made because someone is stupid. Usually they think they're being clever."

"But they're not being clever," Casper said. "I mean, if you were using math to cover up something, then the math should work, right?"

"I would think so," I said, "but most people don't know how to cover their tracks very well. Even the ones who do make mistakes. I can usually find those too. It just takes some digging."

She squeezed the laptop even harder. "Why would you do that?"

"Dig?" I asked. "People think something's fishy, so they ask me to look. I finally got certified so that I can testify in court if I have to."

"When people hit other people?" she asked.

"When they embezzle," I said. "Other people testify about the hitting, usually. Finding embezzlers—thieves— is more of a specialized skill."

She grunted, as if the information was important to her. Her gaze met mine, her frown intense, and then she moved forward swiftly, setting the laptop on my desk. She opened the laptop and tapped the keyboard to bring it out of sleep mode.

"Does this look like stealing to you?" she asked.

I peered at my own program, saw a lot of red where the numbers didn't compute, and then I scrolled through everything. The source for the numbers had come off Casper's thumb drive, but the label on the files wasn't hers.

It was for the shelter.

"Did you tell Reverend Harvey about this?" I asked without looking at her, wondering if that was a bulldozer question.

"Once," she said, sounding sad and furious at the same time. "Just once."

***

It took a special kind of arrogance to embezzle from a nonprofit. It took an even higher degree of arrogance to embezzle from a nonprofit that helped homeless people. It took the highest degree of arrogance to embezzle from a nonprofit that helped homeless people in the name of the Lord.

I decided then and there to wear my Vote Cthulu For God t-shirt in the morning.

But that was the only coherent thought I had. That, and remembering to pay the pizza delivery guy. The rest of the evening, Casper and I went through the shelter's finances, and both of us got pissed off.

Casper had amazing math skills. She had even better computer skills. She suggested a tweak on my program that improved both its entertainment value and its speed.

We didn't even notice when Paladin arrived. She stood behind us long enough to eat half a piece of cold pizza before clearing her throat.

"I see you two hit it off," she said in a self-satisfied tone.

She had scrubbed off the glitter makeup, and she was wearing black jeans and a Kirk/Spock For President t-shirt that dated from 1992. She had removed the wig but had forgotten to comb her short hair, so it stood up in spikes. Or maybe she had done that on purpose, just to rebel against the girl clothes she had worn earlier.

"How'd the gala go?" I asked.

She shrugged. "I got everyone there. We raised funds. We ate weird stuff—or they did. I didn't touch most of it. Then I drove them back and came here."

Casper hadn't even said hello to her. In fact, Casper was hunched forward in her attempting-to-be-invisible posture.

"Can I talk to you?" I said to Paladin.

Casper gave me a sideways glance filled with worry. I nodded to her, and gave her a small okay sign with my thumb and forefinger. I hid the gesture behind my squishy stomach.

Casper nodded once and returned to her invisible pose.

"Okay," Paladin said, and led me to the far side of the room.

"You didn't care about babysitting," I said. "You wanted me to see Casper's files."

Paladin raised her eyebrows. "There are files?"

"Stop it," I said. "You're not very good at games. You know there are files."

"Well?" she asked.

"Well, Casper stumbled on something major," I said, and told Paladin everything, including the fact that Casper had gone to Reverend Harvey and Harvey had hit her.

"I know it," Paladin said fiercely. "I found her crying in the ladies room, but she wouldn't tell me what was going on. That's when I thought of you."

"That was just today?" I asked.

Paladin nodded.

"She'd been in the ladies room all day?"

"I didn't know where else to hide her," Paladin said. "Harvey was mad, but he wouldn't say why, and I knew that Casper had been trying to set up the books as a favor to him for letting her stay at the shelter…"

Paladin's voice drifted off. She was telling me something she shouldn't.

"You may as well tell me the rest," I said.

She shrugged—just like Casper did. "You know the story. It's common since 2009. Parents lost their house, started into drugs, and Casper was too smart for that. So she dodged the system by staying in school and sleeping in different shelters. Reverend Harvey figured it out, and he told her she could stay there, if she helped out. I think he was sincere. He has a good side. It's confusing."

"Because he has sticky fingers," I said.

She nodded.

"I did some digging," I said. "He's got a history of doing this. He makes people love him so they trust him, and give a lot of money. Then he gets a new job offer somewhere else, and when the embezzlement gets discovered a year or so down the road, everyone is unwilling to believe he's a bad guy, so they don't report him."

"Bastard," Paladin said. "It doesn't explain why he hit her."

"Yes, it does," I said. "She discovered the con too early. Guys like him are dangerous when they get caught."

Paladin narrowed her eyes and studied me. Then she paled as she understood what I wasn't saying. "You mean he could've killed her."

I didn't nod. I didn't know if Casper could hear us. But Paladin saw the look in my eyes. She knew.

"The thing I don't get," I said, "is why you didn't just tell me. I'd've gone over the books."

"Would you have talked to her?" Then she answered for me. "Of course not. You 'don't do' children."

"What's so important about talking to her?" I asked. "I would have helped."

"There's a boarding school here for really really bright kids. They're looking for math specialists in general, girls in particular. It's expensive."

"I'd've paid without these machinations," I said.

"I know that," Paladin said. "But I can get money anywhere. What she needs is a sponsor."

And I wouldn't have sponsored her without knowing her. Paladin had me figured out better than I thought.

"That's a pretty subtle maneuver for a bulldozer," I said.

"It wasn't a maneuver," Paladin said. "It was a trick. You'll note I didn't bring you Krispy Kremes tonight."

It took me a minute to realize that she was both punning and she was serious.

"No treat, huh?" I asked. "Isn't it supposed to work that if I don't give you a treat, then you play a trick on me?"

She waved her hand in dismissal. "You get the idea," she said. "So…you'll sponsor her?"

Near my desk, I saw a too-thin body tense. Casper *was* listening.

"Why don't you? You're a relative of hers, right?" I asked.

"No," Paladin said, blinking at me in confusion. "I don't have relatives."

"Like you don't have friends?" I asked.

"No," Paladin said in annoyance. "Like everyone who is related to me is gone. Why would you think that, anyway?"

I glanced at Casper, who looked as confused about my question as Paladin did. Apparently they had no idea how similar they were.

It was finally my turn to shrug. "I don't know. She has your ears."

Paladin's right hand went to her ear. "Lots of people have pointed ears, Spade," she said. "Vulcans do."

"Vulcans aren't real," I said, but then I glanced at Casper. She was more Vulcan than bulldozer. Smart and logical and impatient with those who weren't, even though she tried not to be. And she didn't understand the anger at something presented with logic.

She wasn't made for the streets. She was made for a boarding school that specialized in math and science.

"I'll sponsor her," I said. "But she might have to testify."

"You're calling the cops?" Paladin asked.

"When Casper and I are done compiling the evidence," I said. "You'll have to be on protection duty until then."

Paladin smiled. It made her eyes sparkle. "I can do that," she said.

She parked herself near the door and finished off the pizza while Casper and I dug into the numbers. Other people came and went. The awards got engraved with the wrong names, Betty Jo registered her disapproval one last time to Doris, and I handed over the organized books to next year's convention chair—a guy who probably wouldn't survive the winter.

Alternate Pro-Con went on without me. Halloween passed into All Saints Day and someone dropped extra candy in Ops. Around six a.m., I remembered to shower and put on my Cthulu t-shirt.

And then, when the convention was finally over, I dressed like a real person. I went with Paladin and Casper to the boarding school, feeling less fish-out-of-watery than usual. We took care of the application, the fees, and all the paperwork. A few extra dollars expedited Casper's acceptance—not because she couldn't have gotten in on her own, but because she needed someplace to sleep, and I made sure the boarding school wouldn't waste precious time tracking down her deadbeat parents.

Then the three of us went to the police department, with Casper's evidence, my forensic accountant bona fides, and Paladin's fierceness. The police agreed to arrest Reverend Harvey on the QT, so that the shelter could continue.

And, as I drove us back to the hotel where the con com was disassembling this year's Alternate Pro-Con, I realized that I much preferred my world to Paladin's. In my world, people complained about a rigged award and no one hit anyone and everybody had a home as well as a family, even if that family only got together for an extended weekend in a strange hotel in a strange city.

Even if that family was annoying and difficult and refused to dress up on Halloween.

I didn't mention that to Paladin, although I knew she felt the same. Because as we walked back toward Ops, which was now just a hotel conference space with my Tower of Terror and chair inside, she said softly, "I hate it when a convention is over."

"Yeah," I said. "Me too."

"You said this isn't a real one," Casper piped up from behind me. "I want to go to a real one."

I glanced at Paladin. She half-smiled.

"I promise," she said, "we'll take you to the next real one that comes to town."

"You better," Casper said, sounding more like Paladin than either of them knew. Then Casper put her hand over mouth, realizing that she had spoken out loud.

"We will," I said. "I promise."

"And Spade always keeps his promises," Paladin said.

Her words made me smile. I was surprised that she'd noticed. Or maybe I wasn't. For a bulldozer, she saw me pretty clearly.

Maybe I wasn't as subtle as I thought.

ABOUT THE AUTHOR

USA Today bestselling author Kristine Kathryn Rusch writes in almost every genre. Generally, she uses her real name (Rusch) for most of her writing. Under that name, she publishes bestselling science fiction and fantasy, award-winning mysteries, acclaimed mainstream fiction, controversial nonfiction, and the occasional romance. Her novels have made bestseller lists around the world and her short fiction has appeared in eighteen best of the year collections. She has won more than twenty-five awards for her fiction, including the Hugo, *Le Prix Imaginales,* the *Asimov's* Readers Choice award, and the *Ellery Queen Mystery Magazine* Readers Choice Award.

To keep up with everything she does, go to kriswrites.com. To track her many pen names and series, see their individual websites (krisnelscott.com, kristinegrayson.com, krisdelake.com, retrievalartist.com, divingintothewreck.com, fictionriver.com). She lives and occasionally sleeps in Oregon.

Want to read more stories by Kristine Kathryn Rusch?
Try the award-winning sf thriller Retrieval Artist
series, starting with the first novel,
The Disappeared, on sale now.